ECHOES

ECHOES

ECHOES

Dennis Barone

POTES & POETS PRESS

ELMWOOD, CONNECTICUT

1997

The author is grateful to the following publications in which some of this work originally appeared: *Chain, Confrontation, House Organ, Indefinite Space, Juxta, Open 24 Hours, Poetic Briefs,* and *Rhizome.* Thanks also go to Jonathan Brannen (Standing Stones) for publishing some of these pieces in the chapbook *The Masque Resumed* and to John Byrum (Generator) for publishing others in *A Matter of Habit,* and to Peter Ganick (Potes & Poets) for publishing *With a Thud* as an *hors de commerce.*

ISBN: 0-937013-75-7

Typesetting by Guy Bennett
Cover art: Tim Cunard, *the act of bringing forth ordered existence* (detail)

Contents

With a Thud

HIS PIPE LIT, he looked out the window through the fog toward the castle. A beacon was his pipe. Lighting it and relighting it, it was a definite sign. Another human, nevertheless, abundantly lines the story to ask what is particular about pride. News and letters could be exchanged by a salesman or anyone, but is this all at the climax? Like most of the stories and all men who say *so help me heaven* the seven evangelists anchored the ship to remove the line. The bloody deed was changed as before.

He would let them go and both of them called all night and turmoil ensued. "It's all a poor substitute at best," he said sadly. Quite conceivably it was somehow solidified for his sense of familiarity. To smile and act as if his rage continued began to hold the keepers of government to a half-dozen over there of your class. Then again, even art gets all these people grieved or else he made himself believe that it was magnificently convenient to people who pretended to know.

All night a finger here against the smiling innocence of the company at last incensed. He answered: "on this head no small cut at the bottom." But no good luck came and at all events it seemed obscurely to test the weakness that one heard would uplift the immediate. A silence, a few moments of speaking, of pointing toward the canvas screen and again they gazed at the part a splinter lived where the pine tree fell, a specimen of epitaphs.

After all, others escape from this consuming rage. That's why he hadn't walked over to the subway. New York seemed gray and opalescent. Dawn was breaking. Until now he had to laugh under the lights while the door bolted behind an island of despair. In the silence he became aware of a tense whispering and struggles and exultations, a rude signal of some dying heart. He thought that the silences drew the fundamental honesty along a wild road, a deep romantic finality.

Yes, they were sitting opposite each other in returning to that side of the designs. The whole party will show the least creature a small, round island among the remnants of faith. Yet, lockjawed in all the swift refreshment, it became anathema to every still eye. The history of this crafty mirage, this self-transforming blank cut neatly in some collections of eaves, of any old barn or abbey on the other side. It was a song, a road, an evil moon, a rhyme. In mid-August he produced a folded paper from his pocket and disagreed violently. He called on the phone: "Uh-huh." But there had been for a moment a photograph nestled close to him.

Some months before he glanced, almost glared, at his baskets of fish and went through the corridors in quest of something to drive away the passion he seemed to be turning to and fro, erring as to the manner that object unhinged. In fact, he had vigilance against relapse. He had seen the noisy man in the background, the head-waiter's exaggerated courtesy and threw himself on the bed when his eyes behaved so amazingly. The row of bottles, the pillows, the end. "I can't work or eat or sleep," he began. "I saw you."

This has nothing to do with will power. It was a poem written at school to the elderly aunt who guilelessly allowed rest periods one day and then suggested that any conception of prestige would only prove a somber background for the dissection that they discussed with joy. He was delirious. Down the long street the cushions moved continuously. He was rather glad to walk into the living room. They told him to come up. Somehow the early wind stirred those poor birds with a single soul, stirred a broken fender half delirious and calling, "Come on, that's rather hard." It was just as he had realized it would be, only he felt languid and to his surprise, he dreamed the image of an elm. Anywhere is everywhere, a repeatable format. Nothing can be done without a series of successful experiments, without a peep or a pipe.

Pia at Play

THE FIRST STAGE OF PLAY is a sort of consciousness with regard to the circle. Next, they begin to thumb cumulative repetition with significant failures. The essential thing is the following subject, the fact of discovered chance. It is very difficult to fix, as we have seen, but a search for the schemata only confirms the searching. The only present able to hold, half closes. It is not difficult to note the moment the sheets succeed in the visual field. From this date on the eye resists everything. Already the hand takes hold. Contrary to the random stages in effect, Pia touched all without trying to reach outside the represented objects, without perceiving her hands, without that evening or the following day. The only limitation which still exists is thus pulling them to the same behavior as the right hand directed. Eyes blink. But a moment later, spontaneously, she looks intellectual, so remote from the wood of the stick toys, the things themselves which swing and constitute these relations in the same way that the facts assimilate the sensorial. Moreover, there no longer remains a tin box placed by the strings she made to succeed the power seated in the elementary paragraphs. During every act as complex as that she closes the distance, brings this discovery to the child. Here are the facts: the handkerchief folded; six days later there is only a brush outstretched on the pail. We fall back between the bars and into the former mistakes. Pia remains, perhaps intentionally, incorrect. All that pulls at the lid tries the chain a second time after having disengaged the ring. All the combinations seem very plastic. The situation is so peculiar to the mobile elements of experience that now in the course of development intelligence is granted a self-explanatory realism. He remembered her in essays he wrote at college. He always aspired to fame. So, too, Pia. They differed. In fact, while writing he resisted a brief hysteria and suffered bitter words he doubtless had promised to return to his experts. The recipients looked upon this world as embroiled in a conflict of arms. But here we come upon the little problem that all this completed: the spine does not bend. He turned to Pia then, flipping through the pages in his book, a movement that has gone before as a warning to himself. A concrete expression tidied up the misgivings for a while. A young man dreams that the hero actually plays the least active part. We appear to give something up in those obsessive acts. Meanwhile, Pia proposed the following: the blind spot, the whole wave, the only solution to a vexing problem, Alabama, Mississippi, Florida.

The Shore

BIR-HAKEIM is a stop on the Paris Metro, though it could be something else, too. For example, think of all the things trees can be. Think of the word "note" because it is between memo and letter. It was not a poet who first killed animals of considerable size by means of electricity. Begin then to divide ice with shrill notes, shape ice into continents and where will be the divisions? Then suddenly in the community center where the scene at last is variable they developed a freshness, a personal accent and wit. What was lacking was atmosphere, a trade. There was an impulse to use the absence of our landscape in that year to shape the things and the people in this emptiness. The essence of the place as they had discovered it revealed to them its physical environment, our protagonist. Compromise between those images had been rendered upward in the service of intention. Two-dimensional, immaterial flat pattern of the untrained, the real sitter, thought becomes sympathetic, rejected: the arabesque of the suit. These feelings seem impersonal. The possibility of finding a different result interposed the picture in the mind. Such lines, though they arise from fixed knowledge, direct observation to bear on a single picture.

You will have to pay a tax. Ask for a book called *The Traveler's Companion*. It's a good idea to avoid obsession. Since the process may take several weeks, pause for another dial tone and then continue. You can save money, the best cash. A thrill of hope went over the change that had been coming. "It's only that I can't get through!" His life apart from her – a clan-forming thing – could not, as often was the case, be a confession. In a barn the wheat was terrible. In this moment of drunkenness in fairyland so few have any respect for the world, laborers and all. You know that his secret changed to something with a little more push and verve about it. He had slept, his head just behind the taxi-man. The tendernesses learned are bankrupt. His voice was shaking, he used lists, a parody. Live well. The thought remains his biography where he stands. He chose abandonment. Nothing can be more formless. People forget the enigmatic. His experience is always our own. A man writes a book, a leaf of impressions, in the very same prose you lift. Who set you up for reproach? No trifle, the feelings of the hero guide great affections. Sacredness teaches calamity, elemental power, the sight of buildings, the soul of this faith. In the tedious egotism of knowing, you must be necessary; a sore to imitate. Who was it refused to violate the conclusion because he was distracted by Shakespeare? Passages are often miraculous. The problem is in a certain respect the truest expositor of the practice of thought, the passion of the eye afloat. Hence, the first effort of thought tends to shake our faith in the accuracy of the truth which it illustrates in every character. An interpreter considered every appearance, if traced to its root, in love and incessantly into each other's hands for this delight. We return to the sublime, the beast rushed to completion.

He doubted the old discovery. Perhaps the mistake was that the arrangement required him to live up to his responsibilities. Now he thought of obligation, never taking his eyes off the pine trees – at least, calling to all. Yet, he had lost good luck again; water-courses and stones unravel things step by step. It was high tide. Something had happened. All over the world money belonged to boys like you. I wanted nothing. I lived with that kind of life and that pleased him, too. A blue sky rose gradually from the hardest of all starts. There is evidence on every hand that the little new moon had been used for a stronghold away from their dwellings. The river had kept it preserved in amber, guarded by cliffs, something like that jumble of anything so pure as sculpture. It was nothing. The hand becomes the habit in your mind, in another person's shelter. Everything seemed insupportable: the new commercialism, the pillow at night, the jewelers in a boat, the air above him, the hand and my preferences. The horse was gone, a part of consciousness itself, a walled-in garden.

Down and down, lines added for production. If a man professed beliefs, delivered and published a prepared statement, a series of short films, praises will never incur guilt. The attack is made, resigning life and the temper of swords. A proof of courage requires war to render obedience to those doctrines that deal with frail, fallen spears. Shining lights so distracted the world that war was thought best for him and the tokens it bears of courage likewise let the manner promote no authority for that purpose. A crime if it be necessary to sweep all before them, to expect a crop before the end of it. I consider one objection more: beggary. Things excite you. Our land mourns.

The entire town will talk more of private interest, and protesting, a riot broke out. Even in documents this privatism doomed them, eloquence fails, borrowed. The thinness of reward did not mean they lived as fanatics, the body sold back to us. It does not help us to know anything of modern science and technology. We have not replaced them. The absence of a message, facts, the objects themselves hold the issues in prose. We could expect that utterance brings everything together. The fence is what we mean – psychoanalytically.

Violence rationalized beyond the door, eyes become passageways. What is situated? This time is clearly meant to be seen as the fault of the literal. Strong willed, the honest voices' extreme identity on the point of breaking too. They have gained a necessary object: the resolution of the enigma. Withhold the pier only the father holds. This includes the interruptions, the structure of spectacle. If only you could fly, then there would be no question of the purpose balloons serve: to move beyond the wall, to be a part of that garden and all that we had formerly conquered against the glass airplane.

The Broken Spine

JULY IMPOSTOR. Do you think we called you too late? What was the moment to dart the pavements in the ensuing silence like a first authentic experience doing folded in the upper right hand corner of the page? People wore clothes of that sort and yet she didn't mind soiled sheets and charred tabletops. Not at all. The thing now was to get hold of her and coach her in her story before it was too late.

Just then she reappeared, not for the first time, either. She couldn't get away from their culture. The ride got tied up with snags about how it helps to call "trying to do the right thing" horrible. Without even telling them, smoking vigorously of course, she realized at once that her mind had been made up as soon as she decided to make the journey. She went back to the right road, which is a very pleasant one.

Backwards: the browning age of the loose sheet, the folded page, the unmarked passage in her unfinished letter – "*last summer.*" Finally, it was privilege, not neglect that decided it. It appeared plainly after all, the ruddy volumes, for the most part, complete. She wore many jewels for the pleasure of her muses then. Error is all to blame for the page left unbound, for what grace remained in her heart: its power the concessions it made.

Given all these careers she had there is something that a more serious relationship would have served to contrast to that old stereotype of the doughty account and its reasons for failure. The names run literally into the dozens and it is true that certain connotations for the whole community widened steadily as the years passed. Fifteen to twenty, about twenty, joined the short-lived Dominion under her control in the spring of that final year. As long as there was space for both the members and the townspeople, even the most traumatic events never made sacrifice necessary. It should be possible, after all, to mitigate costs woven into the pattern of our daily lives. What would it mean in hospitals, clinics, outpatient facilities when she hands him her bread? Options for the career soldier broadened because volunteer tutors from the Dominion instructed them in building projects ranging from distant resorts to local park facilities. How is enjoyment in this to be explained? They are healthier and happier even if this is too late, even if there is no more space. For the man at the door still asked for the names of all the people living here.

Life in the City

NEW YORK NEVER SLEEPS. She ties her hair and bides her time. She knows all the answers. New York is a sister, a mother, a wife, a daughter. She has seven children and lives on the Lower East Side. New York crosses the street and when she does so she is never happy. This is the story of New York.

Late in August, early in September; high above her apartment set low beneath the bridge, New York breathes one long sustained breath of contentment. This is the day that she will do it, she says perspiring. She will soon unhinge herself from the hook by the door, she will soon stop the traffic and make rain fall from the sky. She is New York and she is strong and powerful.

She has a dog named La Guardia. He is little and pugnacious, little and loud. New York does not know what kind of dog La Guardia is. She found him at the pound. She took La Guardia home after he licked her hand. To this day, there is nothing that La Guardia so loves as to lick New York's hand. New York has everything in abundance, including licks from little and loud La Guardia who barks all the time.

New York constantly worries about running out of time and of having nowhere to go. New York is nothing but a worry-wart. New York can't ever find what she wants at the grocery store when she wants it. This, she decides, is life in the city.

My First Step

WHAT IS AN EPIGRAPH? How is this one? Where is it from and why? Why begin and end with "rebuild the dog"? English soldiers' moral responsibility changes, but not the ethics of those they use. Car fenders accept the innocent best example. Besides, that innocence is only feigned. They will travel to get away from wives. Contemporary America became happy in two ways. What finally will happen to it? What is the central irony? What lesson will the narrator learn? Will this alleviate his dim outlook?

The literal meaning of words is disregarded in order to show or imply a relationship between diverse things. Filler paper and Lady Capulet, for example. "It seems she hangs upon the cheek of night," etc. "Snapped" versus "said angrily," etc. Or "I cursed like hell" versus "I was absolutely horrified," etc. Now for that slice of sausage, the real stuff.

The two most obvious solutions to the logistic problems appeared in the early 1830s. Thereupon, Achilles refused to fight and sulked in his tent. After much pleading, the poem finished. There were three main threads to the story. Penelope held many suitors at bay. Discuss examples.

Control exists in access to housing figures. How does virtue work in autobiography? Are we then a civilization without any cultures? Strangers, yes, and our gay city lacks, in one of the most respectable parts of the city, nightly pocket companions. The accommodation has a few boarders; all good and safe, second class. In Maple Street we have no objection to make her Palace of Love attractive. A good many have bought our book. Try to see that place, that place would be unbearable. Heisler went on to make *Storm Warning*.

It took time to get from the arrow to the diamond. We have had witnesses of bad weather in all seasons. The first step is always the hardest. Like a rock. The southwest rock, Blue Mesa, not exactly the moon, but better. Couldn't get it anywhere. Maybe in the summer, in the room – questions, explorations, viewpoints – expose the need (the rock), fulfill the need. Is there a need? For what? The poundage: cake, spaghetti. Coincide. Climb.

Take corn beef out. (Self-censorship.) Convert outsiders into insiders. (Rhetoric.) Aid industry to ally agitation: "I know you so well." Men are under the command of a sort of minority report, the majority report having been sent in by MGM. It is never either/or, but it is always *the extent to which*. Clearly.

But the things which both choose to talk about are the same things: cars, living rooms, mothers. We have just seen the film about these same things. At a very young age a Christmas tree gets dressed up, then stripped bare. Still in the living room there are no monsters.

In New York, as in London and Paris, a number of artists of all sorts thought that they could part the active themes of the self-apparent. The whim and whistle of the machine becomes as beautiful as a miracle. Freud said that how does a thing become conscious would be more advantageously stated how does a thing become thought. *Mise-en-scène* is no cure for montage.

There are no bullets in this accent, but the conditions are real. The present order must convince us that what is unrealizable in the present order is unrealizable in any order. Come to grips with it if you think determinism is needlessly arbitrary.

It is here. "All you can expect from life is an apology for all the things you'll never get." Be specific. Social order exists. It is breathless in these terms. What is the external criteria? The future? I'm interested in it. Choice is always tempered by chance. A girl with a gun he didn't want. Pictures. Hand out the ammunition. Tripod. Adderly. Nine minute title. Fourth. Blue raincoat. Street. Sounds. Italian folk song of great joy. Three walls, color. Zoom on blue Luger. Titles. Window shots. Pan bridge. Begin and end. Thirty feet. Set on tripod as slides. Exposure checked. Bright. South to north. Second roll. Thirty-seven feet. Zoom on blue coat. Cut. Start again. Gone clear, no blue. Hold and cut. Third roll. Forty-two feet. Northwest corner. Sunglasses on turn. Blue and southeast corner. Look and see Luger rise. End.

Starker: Stone-Light

As it stands the context shows the first dialogue is interrupted and to the end of the reading is clearly incorrect. Although an error, the death referred to can be justified but the knowledge referred to would have created a possible remedy. Members of the family benefit as well as render the test parallel with the word since not claiming possible artifices omitted in an earlier description. The time of two distinct sciences is not just an error for accomplishing a plausible lifeless scene. In the city the latter is genuine. As it stands the meaning seems to be skipped, especially in this lack of agreement which follows in this sense the error on its own instance. Likewise, employment terminates ignominious emendations. Exhilaration occurred, putting myself across a glancing moment. Conspicuous were we controlling analogous answers. I was corrosive. I shuddered, attendant. Considerations receive enough acts, passions might college food. However, books recollected the city coming from guilt particular. Probably despised. Meanwhile tranquillity threaded excursions' lasciviousness. Ignorance engaged. Intoxication: you place, I come if the word happens. Both omit hereafter himself. Short-sighted, somewhat penniless, as it stands, nothing breakfasted banknotes. Irksome blood-stained fashion without carefully toilsome cheerfulness withdrew forever honorable rendezvous. Darksome, myself steadfast, three-fourths barefoot, something hasty, artless, gentleman, ill-humored – nothing headlong without all-absorbing half-decayed tyger-like self-destruction. Henceforth hopeless street door list not the woebegone nothing without. Decisions and authority revisit window-shutters raised whenever the usual titles appear in a given entry. The city celebrity with a candle directs reason. A ploughman transacts safer reserve delivered along with hues momentarily awake. Darkness, a passion not of some hand will be surveyed. This plot inconveniences an hour sunk. It was gloom his eyes should hope. Poverty, an acquaintance, hastened malignant obscurity. My apprehension freed me. Regard my eyes. Retreat. Was not a husband informed tonight to seclude the heart of shuddered property? This city directed an inexplicable sum to crime. Whatever distant chief ill foot stairs, a forest sisters chance. Far off a regret threw respiration in the excited ill treatment warm and dry. In some way perhaps he was the father of fortune. Dying, he was able. Both replaced malaise, plough-land and meadow saying, "subsistence." Anger bid incidents balk. Her hazard a mantle piece. Me? Her friendlessness pressed. My life hastened tumult. Ill-treated, the emissaries hastened the post. That astonishing interview accomplished your wishes. Tomorrow what kind lodging by these sheets leads me to her own place following footsteps. Hope and dream, a surprise bank notes a proposal. Strange report. As it stands, this note accompanied thought snatched in headlines, answered in lost copies. Missing these chapters, the wave displaced caution. A possible child perhaps. A ploughman bound inquires and sensed absurd information. As it stands, terms perverse variation sprung to future curiosity a bar, toll-gatherer entitled! He inquires, encourages, inquires. The willing however pump trousers. Knee unbound, unpracticed bachelor repeated dinner-hour uneasiness. Dejection shrouded appearances. As it stands, the glances opened the following.

Two Dogs of Empiricism

THE PROBLEM OF MEANING, particularly as involved in the notion of an analytic statement. The notion of commitment, particularly as involved in the problem of universals. This formulation has two shortcomings. The present and necessary function of poetry is transformation. In addition, there is the paper, the subsequent image. The whole is more than the sum of its parts. Its shadow is cut with white birds in mind.

I am exaggerating here. Now whether or not this is true, imagine that the orientation of a field operates secretly. The illusion of motion is not static as a painting. Functions of the body are realized out of parts of the body. These are not words of obfuscation, but of clarification.

Where there is no symmetry there can be no rest. Putting these two together we have tension and calmness. This deduced possibility emerged purely from the evident. There is the heightening effect of jewelry and other objects being tossed on the bed. Then, almost like a photo on the bed, but tactile, too, are clothes crumpled in a setting of rock, weed, and sand. I don't remember.

In the iris shot a kiss is almost felt upon the cheek. The track fades as he remembers that remembrance, even such simple things as the boy and his older brother. Finally, art's task is to parallel the drama and the tension of the other. There is even a chase in the hall. I begin to stumble. It immediately became law.

It is precisely this embeddedness that makes the revolution of the morning the menu of lunch. Mother Courage must realize the error of her ways for the play to achieve its ends. After all, the world is what it is becoming. If you want to know if what you are doing is OK, just ask.

The son of a doctor in government service decided to become a doctor, too. He became involved in radical politics. He died shortly after he started. It appears that he did not think of puppet-plays or iron-clad laws. Parade-horses cannot be mentioned, nor the sight of blood. This formulation has two shortcomings. Society has neither eyes nor ears for it. At last, it has either married or shot itself dead. How sweet the sound. They will cry out that it was ideal. Then the court learned that he had been hearing noises. The idea behind the idea co-exists in each movement. Too coincidental? His mother had been his middle-class father's second wife, a servant girl whom he had married after making her pregnant. He painted, too. The irrational differences dropped out of the unconscious.

On the slight groundwork of reality, imagination spins. Two dogs in Hume's distinction between truths of reason and truths of fact. The orphanage merged into poetic devices but gradually veered toward historical subjects. This leads to expressionism, but that's for another day.

Attached to the court, a tender and melancholy lyricist marred these native incarnations of success. Oblique characters of absolute failure must act by the urgencies of consciousness like a friend, simple as life is.

In solitude and in silence, the poet cannot evoke the tragic image that has stirred the drawing-room. One realized anew vast passions. The servant-girls in the kitchen were serious and also complete. Thirty-eight executed.

This formulation has two shortcomings. A man lives. There arises a crisis. How does he react to it? The mask is often dropped and then resumed. Remedy both at once in the space between art and actuality. Age is fixed. He enters scenes to remain fixed, but others don't take him seriously. The tyranny of actions taken presents events as in the past. Two vertical posts did not attract too much attention.

To see, not necessarily to please, that beauty apart from deeds, the texture of one. This formulation, particularly, has two short-comings.

No Answer

The Dream of Reason breeds monsters.
—GOYA

*The highest, most perfect life is a life of
pure vegetation.*
—SCHLEGEL

" 'WHEN I SEE a beautiful Building of exact Order and Proportion taken down,' " Constance Wright said quoting at this point from Henry Felton's *A Dissertation on Reading the Classics and Forming a Just Style*, " 'and the different Materials laid together by themselves, it putteth me in mind of these Common-Place Men.' "

Wright asserted that ornament is to architecture as rhetoric is to writing and had spent the last half hour quoting from a variety of Enlightenment texts – both British and Continental – to illustrate this analogy. Furthermore, she theorized that if each religion is its own rhetoric, then there should be differences between the books and buildings of different religious groups and if verbal and physical structures are similar expressions of the same system, then when writing changes there should be an equivalent and parallel change in architecture.

R. Bowdler Sharpe, the ornithologist, sat unimpressed. Brandini steamed. Wright continued: " 'The Materials are certainly very good, but they understand not the Rules of Architecture so well, as to form them into just and masterly Proportions any more: And yet how beautiful would they stand in another Model upon another Plan!' "

She then wanted to show a slide of George J. Henkel's house described by William Tennis in George Fisher's *The American Instruc-*

tor as "unsurpassed on this side of the Atlantic" (at the moment, mid-sea, an inaccuracy) "in point of elegance of design and perfection of workmanship" and as "so completely Parisian that we could scarcely believe it was made in this country" to show an important connection between "eloquence of design" and eloquence as the art of speaking well on any subject in order to please, to instruct, or to persuade and to pose the rhetorical question to her audience, "how does a building speak?" But the slide in the tray did not correspond to the order of her talk and at this moment instead of the gaudy gilt mansard, everyone saw, but barely, a dimly lit gothic scene depicting a prison of castellated design illuminated, apparently, by the lamp held by a short, stocky jailer.

Brandini, rudely, laughed. Constance, as ever, went on. She quoted from Penn's *Fruits of Solitude*: " '… things are still to be preferred. Children had rather be making of tools, and instruments of play; shaping, drawing, framing, and building, & c. than getting some rules of propriety of speech by heart …'" She was about to explain the way in which Boileau had said that words are things and so are bricks and if bricks are the blocks of construction then words are the cement of argument, but just at that moment Constance looked up, turned toward the screen and away from her audience, spoke toward the screen as follows: "I do not have the same experience in these matters as my colleague Aldo Brandini. How excellently he runs a projector. It is a marvel, indeed." Then, turning back toward the audience, with no modulation of voice so that whereas only half of the audience heard her comment about Brandini everyone heard her say, "Why didn't someone say something? Why didn't someone tell me I had the wrong slide up?" She paused a moment and then added, from Felton again, " 'I can compare such Productions to nothing but rich Pieces of Patch-work, sewed together with Patch-thread!' " Some (those nearest the front of the hall) thought that she referred to Brandini and his slide trays, some thought it a humorous comment on her present mix-up, but most thought it some sort of insult to themselves for surely they were all having trouble following the thread that sewed together the divisions and sub-divisions of her talk. At just that instant a wave of extraordinary size rocked the ship and Wright stumbled. Some thought the stumble divine, her comeuppance. If only Aldo had been given more time, they thought.

"Friends," Constance said steadying herself, "Verbal and physical structures are similar expressions of the same system. Systems will differ in two ways: time and place. Hence, every age has its peculiar mode; every place has its common habits in books as well as buildings. And what we have observed this evening is the commonality of these common habits. The Messieurs Du Port Royal spoke not only of 'the style of each Age,' but also of the way 'we know not only the Humour of a Man by his Style, but also his Country.'"

As Wright spoke Brandini kept pushing his glasses up and down his nose. He looked serious. Then he thought to himself, "what if this constant up and down movement elongates my nose?" He desisted with the glasses. Carefully, without drawing attention to himself, he looked at his watch. 9:30. Although he had spoken for ninety-minutes and Wright just now had surpassed thirty, he felt the length of her talk intolerable, her drift incomprehensible. He gave it another try, listened once again as she quoted from Quintillian's *Institutes of Eloquence* as translated by William Guthrie, 1756: " 'it is not enough for one who undertakes a Building to bring together his Stones, his Materials, and every thing that is proper for carrying it on, unless the Whole is disposed of, and conducted, by the Skill of an able Architect; so, in the Study of Eloquence, it is not enough that a large Mass of Materials be piled and heaped up together, unless *Disposition* shall reduce them into Order, and connect them into strong, but graceful, Uniformity.'" Why does a critic of fiction speak at such length about architecture, Brandini wondered? What business is it of hers? Why doesn't she skip the slides and read us a poem? He mused.

Then she finished, saving her most eloquent lines for her closing: "While we associate the gothic with the efforts of the common man, we associate the classical with a wise and benevolent aristocracy. The ambivalence regarding self-interest on the one hand and public virtue on the other that historians have recently written so much about is still with us – an unresolved contradiction in American culture. Parallel false doors maintain a deceitful harmony. Thank you and goodnight."

"Historians! Historians!" Brandini thought, "how did she get to historians?" Wright's conclusion had completely baffled him. He must have missed something, something important, he thought, while he was playing with his glasses. Meanwhile, it was time to steady himself, to concentrate and focus for the expected questions.

The Captain rose and walked to the front of the hall as the light applause fizzled. He thanked both speakers for a stimulating evening, invited everyone back the following night to hear Robert McCracken Peck present an illustrated lecture entitled "Drawn from Nature: The Extraordinary Bird Books of Jay Gould and His Circle." (Sharpe's eyes lit up at the mention of Peck's program.) The Captain then opened the floor for questions. There were many questions addressed to Aldo Brandini and each questioner began with a compliment to the speaker. Brandini, in turn, first thanked each one for his or her kind words and then succinctly answered the question. Wright received no questions, but she did reply to one addressed to her colleague. She stumbled a bit and finally admitted that the question required a treatise, the variables are innumerable, she said. Brandini then clarified everything in one declarative sentence.

All in all, it was not a successful launch for Constance's speaking career. On the other hand, for Aldo it was another triumph. It disgusted Constance that while she had something unique, original, and serious to say, something which took months to prepare, the audience appreciated Aldo's textbook talk and hated hers. It disgusted Constance that she had prepared her talks during the months prior to leaving port and revised them constantly while on ship. Aldo, on the other hand, did nothing but attend parties before departure and promoted his talks every chance he got since they left. Amazingly, on such a neat, ship-shape ship everywhere one looked there was a poster for Aldo. Come hear Aldo signs were everywhere and everyone flocked to hear him. The night the Nobel Prize economist lectured on changes in the United States economy using a defunct Ford Plant as his example there was hardly a soul present. Constance was there; Sharpe wasn't. It disgusted Constance that Aldo never said anything new. In fact, what she heard tonight she found troublingly familiar. She made a mental note of this fact and vowed to look into the unacknowledged sources of Aldo's talk.

She wasn't scheduled to speak again for a week. Aldo, on the other hand, would speak every night for a week except for the next night, nor would he speak the night that Constance would present the talk she thought potentially her best. She called it, "The Steeple." The pairing she thought could have been better. She would share the stage that night with the acclaimed novelist Myrrh Grove who would read from his new work-in-progress *Metamorphosis*, a story centered on a character who could turn himself inside out through his penis. He becomes a freak in a traveling circus, constantly repeating his bizarre trick over and over again. Eventually, just as audiences begin to tire of him, he falls in love with a trapeze artist who just at that moment was at the height of her career. (Constance thought that this might be the reason behind the pairing – some perceived connection between a steeple and a high wire act.) The real tragedy of Grove's new novel is that the very physical oddity that had provided the freak show character's livelihood makes having sex difficult. This was as far as Grove had gotten at this point. His character still had no name and what he would do to resolve this tragic love story still remained to be worked out in the depths of the genius's imagination. Constance thought it entirely inappropriate that she had been paired with a novelist whose books she had criticized in the past and whose present work she knew had no connection whatsoever to her devoted and diligent search for historical truth.

But who else could she have been paired with on this ship? Certainly not with Sharpe and his whistles and calls. She began to regret this adventure. There was D. Bryan Keith, also known as D. Bryan Fox, the film historian who so loved and treasured *Citizen Kane* that he spoke only with words and phrases from that film. When asked by a waiter one night at dinner if he would like the grilled tuna – "it's very good this evening, Sir" – he assumed a nasal, New York style of speech and attacked the waiter with the line: "Are you being paid for your opinions or for hauling?" Constance found it difficult to imagine a whole lecture composed in such a "patchwork" manner. He had been, however, for several seasons the most popular lecturer other than the great Brandini.

Another possibility would have been Riff Randal, the antiquarian book collector. He had the world's largest collection of first editions of long novels. Something here Constance found profoundly interesting, but it deeply troubled her that RR, as some called him, had never read a single book in his collection: not *Moby-Dick*, not *The Monk*, not *Nicholas Nickleby*, not *War and Peace* – nothing.

Einar Norsen, the scientist who so worshipped technology, would have made a good pairing for Constance regarded her new historical interests as something of a science but Norsen would only speak on a program with other men. He made this stipulation not out of an ancient male chauvinism, but because of a current romantic infatuation. He had fallen in love and he worried that if he lectured on the same bill as a woman his beloved would become insensibly jealous. Yet, at the moment he had not communicated his affections to this woman and so she – whoever she was – was not even aware that she was the orb around which he orbited.

Then there was Hans Atozen, the philosopher, who no one had

seen on ship yet though rumors aplenty circulated about him. Some thought that he had never boarded the ship and rather than cause a ruckus with the passengers the Captain ordered his staff to pretend that the great philosopher remained below deck at work in his cabin around the clock. Others thought that the philosopher practiced nudism and rather than shock the passengers the Captain had locked him in, would keep him under lock and key until the night of his much anticipated first lecture. Some said that the Captain had locked Atozen in his cabin because when he first arrived at the dock he shook hands with the Captain and then told the Captain that he had a lovely, lovely boat and thus with these innocent words he had irrevocably offended the good Captain. Some said Hans Atozen still struggled with the terrible fate of his late brother-in-law Charles F. Richter, the co-inventor of the earthquake measuring system which bears his name, whose personal possessions had recently been destroyed by fire.

Still others said that shortly before departure, shortly after his brother-in-law's double tragedy of death and destruction, the philosopher had gone for a hike in the hills that surround his university in order to calm his mind, to attune himself to life-cycles, nature, and the great flux and flow of the universe. He took a rugged, but well-traveled path. On the way out he noticed the dropping temperature and the rapid, rising waters of the river. He thought nothing of it – the story goes – for several sturdy bridges, such as the one he first crossed, spanned the river. By the time he had nearly completed his loop, the sun had almost set and the temperature had dropped to a barely tolerable degree. When he got to the bridge from which he would have but a short walk to the first of the university buildings, the swiftness of the river startled him so much that he almost failed to observe that all the planks had been removed from the bridge. Some sick, twisted fraternity prank, he thought. Rather than turn back into the approaching dark, he decided to climb across the bridge by way of the support rails and main side spans. He removed his gloves so that he could get a better grip. The steel nearly stung him when he first touched its coldness. Moving around the perpendicular support beams proved an especially difficult task. He tried not to look down for the speed of the surging river he found hypnotic. At one point he stopped and considered dropping one of his gloves in the water so that he could watch the river's might hurry it away. When he reached the other side night had fallen and his hands peculiarly stung him, something like a lot of prickly little bug bites. He joked to himself, "I guess I really have frozen my hands off." As it turned out, according to this story, that is exactly what he had done. So now Hans had no hands and he would not come out of his cabin because he had not yet become accustomed to his new – handless – appearance.

Another rumor had it that Hans wasn't his name anyway. If not handless he was perhaps "Han-less." His real name was Scotty Williams. Yes, he was the fellow who so many years ago had gotten mixed up with the failed plot to kill former President Gerald Ford. Scotty Williams was the young graduate student who accidentally saved Ford's life. Because he did not approve of Ford's pardon of Richard Nixon, he hesitated to shake the former President's hand when he passed Ford on the steps of the Van Pelt Library at the University of Pennsylvania. Ford was coming out of the library and down the stairs as Scotty Williams was going in – thrilling to the words of Emerson and Heidegger that spun in his head. He recognized, of course, the former President, hesitated a moment because of the pardon and because of principle. Ford extended his hand but because Scotty did not immediately offer his hand, Ford did one of his famous stumbles. By then Scotty had extended his hand and grabbed hold of Ford's. At just that moment – as everyone knows – a shot rang out from somewhere in the gothic College Hall directly across the quad from Van Pelt. Scotty – heroically as it turned out – instinctively squeezed Ford's hand as hard as he could and jerked him down hard in the direction that he was already falling. They both rolled down the concrete steps, but suffered no more injury than some cuts and bruises. Scotty became an instant celebrity, but he had to endure weeks of interrogation by the CIA, the NSC, the FBI, and network television. So, he changed his name to Hans Atozen. At least, that's the story. And ever since that time he has been very shy and hence he keeps to his cabin.

One final story had it that Hans Atozen was actually much older, not in his late forties but in his mid-eighties and that in the 1930s he had gone to agricultural school in New Jersey. The Dean befriended this smart but poor young man and let him live for free in a former chicken coop on his farm. In the room that the young man built out of the old chicken coop he hung only a single decoration – a large hammer and sickle banner. Every morning he would ride to the State University in the rumble seat of the Dean's old car. Every day they made this ritual trip together. One day the young man had come down with a sickness that kept even a student so devoted to his studies as he in his room. The Dean checked on his young protégé and then drove off. That was to be the last time they'd speak for on his way home that evening on a dark, icy road the Dean lost control of his old car and died later that night from injuries he sustained when it rolled on top of him. The young man was quite distraught, but soon after his grief subsided a little he realized he now had no where to live and no way to get to school. The Dean's distant relatives in Iowa had decided to sell the farm immediately at a rock bottom price. But then as the lawyer hired by the relatives rummaged through the Dean's papers he discovered that an account had been established for the young student. While it wasn't a fortune by any means, it would pay for his last two years at the University and allow him to move into a room on campus.

He roomed with another student, a naval engineering major. Although they became good friends, they differed in their political views. They'd stay up late at night arguing about FDR beneath the hammer and sickle banner. After graduation the Dean's protégé got a job with the United States Department of Agriculture and later with the United Nations. The Dean would have been so proud of him. The naval engineering major, on the other hand, took a different path. After graduation he started a firm that built room dividers. When the political climate changed in the late forties, early fifties, the young liberal, agriculture specialist found himself under investigation. Apparently, his former college roommate, his friend, had given the FBI his name. That banner and those late night debates came back to haunt him. When Eisenhower became President, before any moderation of the red scare phobia, he lost his job. At this point he became a devoted follower of Reinhold Niebuhr and changed his name.

Finally, there was Jaspar Ponds, the Nobel Prize winning economist. The ship's public relations staff thought it quite a coup to sign Ponds up for the season. But Ponds did not seem in his element on this trip. If the audience had trouble following Constance Wright's arguments regarding rhetoric in writing and ornamentation in architecture, they found Jaspar Pond's words insulting. He began his first shipboard lecture as follows: "Two centuries ago, a former European colony decided to catch up to Europe. It succeeded so well that the United States of America became a monster, in which the taints, the sickness, and the inhumanity of Europe have grown to appalling dimensions."

At his second lecture, his "Ford Plant" talk, much to the complete despair of the public relations staff, there were but a handful of people in the audience. Constance was glad that she had not been paired with Ponds for certainly she'd then give her "Steeple" talk to just two others: Ponds and the ever faithful Captain. Better, she thought, to at least have the crowd that would be there to listen to Grove's penis story.

Ponds had begun his second talk with even more poison for the audience than his first. He said that "the church does not call us to God's ways but to the ways of the master, of the oppressor. And as we know, in this matter many are called but few are chosen." No one could explain Ponds's sea change. What led to the sudden radicalization of this former Reagan administration advisor remained something of a mystery, one which no one on this ship had any interest in solving. If it had been the other way around, if Ponds had been a radical transformed into a supply-side economist then everyone on this ship would want to solve the mystery of such a transformation, bottle the catalyst and infuse it into a nation's drinking water. Such is the complexion of this ship. Then again if Ponds had been known as a radical before boarding ship he would never have been hired for the season.

Ponds continued his second lecture with – as he described it – a little personal anecdote. Out where the Ford Plant used to be there once was a large red barn. On its side in huge white letters someone had painted "Christ Died For Our Sins." He saw these words almost every day as a boy. He left home and did not return for many years. When he returned home as a man all that remained on the barn were two words in light, fading letters: "Christ Died." This anecdote, Ponds said, served as emblematic for his entire talk that evening.

He continued with a story about a princess who wants to visit a prince held captive in a tower. Eventually she gets to go to the tower, sees the prince, and, as her parents feared, falls immediately and passionately in love. The prince's enemies come to the tower to execute him, but before they can do so, the prince and princess jump to their deaths. Then the princess's slave comes to the tower, sees what has happened, climbs to the top of the tower, and jumps to her death. But at the bottom of the tower all three – prince, princess, and slave – start to laugh. Thus, according to Ponds, are class relations undermined.

Next he turned to America again. "It is possible to lose a hoard of money brought to America," he said. "The revisionist historians claim that those who made fortunes in America had a fortune at the outset. No one speaks of those unspeakable misfortunates who instead of doubling substantial resources lost it all. But it did and still does happen. More often than you think. More often than you're told."

He then spoke about a house on a hill, a house of cavernous rooms and mile-long halls, about the death of a child and the death of a parent, about the disintegration of a fortune: a brother of eight marriages, a sister's death, shrinking money all the time, a business begun at the worst possible moment, all this until the roof literally caved in on them after a particularly vicious snowstorm.

This, too, was an emblematic tale. For he moved from faith to fantasy to one particular family to the reality experienced by thousands of workers a short time ago. He spoke of the world's largest single story automotive plant and how it once employed sixteen thousand people. From the top of a nearby hill one could see its massive form sprawl out across a valley, an octopus that one day died. Then the dozers came and reclaimed it: the land, reshaped the land into gardens and reflecting pools. It became a hotel and conference center that employed five-hundred people, most at minimum wage. Then he started to cry and could go no further. If Constance Wright was too rational then Jaspar Ponds was too emotional.

But there was more to life aboard the ship than the lectures. For example, "The Hospital Nurse of Tennessee, A Military Musical of Great Rebelliousness, In Four Acts" would have its revival next week. After a brief stop in port the mail room became a place of heightened activity. Often at such times the Captain would assign extra staff to the task of sorting. The piles sometimes reached floor to ceiling, enough to sink a less sturdy ship it seemed, but eventually it all got sorted, distributed, and gradually answered.

Brandini prepared for his next appearance in his usual way. From sunup to sundown he pasted announcements for his next talk everywhere on the ship. He seemed to have keys for every room, he seemed able to contort his body into the tightest corners, anywhere anyone might possibly pass – there was an Aldo Brandini sign.

Constance Wright had grown accustomed to this madness. Brandini had never read a book in his life, she thought. All he ever did … But although she had begun to ignore these signs something in this one caught her attention. This one had a picture of Brandini, but quite clearly the man pictured and identified as Brandini was not Brandini. Brandini was tall and fat, but the person in the photograph was short and thin. The poster invited passengers and staff to hear all about Aldo's latest discoveries in an illustrated slide lecture and showed a man identified on the poster as Aldo Brandini kneeling in a pit – pith helmet and all – at a Roman archaeological site. This enraged Constance Wright and she brought it to the attention of others. They told her to relax. "Constance, you're too literal," they said.

The night of Constance's "Steeple" lecture had arrived. As it turned out it pleased her immensely to be paired with Myrrh Grove. Even though she had tired her audience that first night, the room was full. Granted, they were all there to hear Grove's freakish tale of genital difficulties and oddities. But, nonetheless, they were there and since she would speak first tonight they'd stay there. She was excited.

Her thesis once again combined a number of disciplines, but this time she focused on a single man rather than an entire culture. She argued that signs – whether physical or verbal – are acts of control or submission. When the colonial American evangelist Samuel Giedion undertook to raise funds for a steeple for his church he did so not as a sign of God's glory on earth but as notification that his congregation had now assumed leadership of the city. Hence, the steeple Giedion had constructed reached higher than any other in the city; the steeple could be seen far out in the river. It was the sign that let all know that they had reached the city, but it also let all who reached it know who controlled it. If this physical sign did not make this clear, Wright went on, then Giedion's challenge, as it was known, certainly did. In his sermons – which in their published versions became the bestsellers of that time, that place – he warned his listeners to be sure that their ministers had abundant heat as well as sufficient skill. Since his skill in classical homily was less than that of neighboring preachers and since his fire burned brighter than all others, he meant that just as his church had the highest steeple and hence commanded all others, so too should his preaching be the most highly regarded and take precedence over all competitors. Wright then showed that in the following decade four out of five city mayors were part of this congregation and across the province during that time the percentage of legislators who practiced this faith drastically increased while the number of legislators who practiced other faiths precipitously declined.

Constance's audience rewarded her initial excitement. The applause, while not energetic, was kind and polite and there were several questions. One person remarked that city churches in the eighteenth century seemed to be analogous to city movie theaters in the twentieth century. Constance complimented the person who made the comment and promised to look into it. She said this even though she thought the man a fool. She had learned a few things about public speaking in the past week. Her excitement had energized her presentation and her emphasis on one man created a sort of character identification for the audience. Even the Captain congratulated her. "Smooth sailing," he said to Constance as he pumped her hand. She felt so good that she told several people at the intermission that like them she too looked forward to Aldo's next talk.

During his illustrated slide lecture on the composer-painter Hugo van Stadt, Brandini said the following: "We see the musician evoking mood and emotion through the painter's palette." This sentence deeply troubled Constance Wright. Although it typified Brandini's style – especially the "We see ..." – she found it surprisingly dreadful and she suspected that she had heard it before or had seen it in print somewhere. All she could hear the remainder of the evening was: "We see the musician evoking mood and emotion through the painter's palette." Over and over no matter what Aldo said she heard the same thing again and again.

By chance after the lecture was over, after the applause had died down, after the questions had been summarily answered Constance discovered herself standing next to Aldo and then shaking his hand. Aldo told the crowd that had gathered about him to excuse Constance's distractedness. She still glowed in the success of her "Steeple" lecture. He added that he had heard all about it and apologized for not being there to share in her triumph. Constance then excused herself and hurried from the hall.

The next morning Constance went directly to the ship's library, a very beautiful room of rosewood paneling, brass knobs, the works. The ship's holdings were especially strong in geography and western art history. She found the catalogue of Hugo van Stadt's only major solo exhibition: a posthumous retrospective at the Williamstown Art Museum in 1928. She flipped through it and very quickly discovered what she thought she would, but what she had hoped she would not. On page thirty-three, adjacent to an illustration of one of his many paintings of his beloved oak trees, she read: "We see the musician evoking mood and emotion through the painter's palette." She knew she need not read anymore. She did not know what to do next for she believed that Aldo Brandini was an institution, a sacred institution and to question his integrity might only serve to ruin her reputation with six more months of sailing yet to go. Smooth sailing it might no longer be.

Constance Wright lived more by idyllic principle than by pragmatic self-interest. For example, even in her "Steeple" lecture she did not give the audience what it wanted to get, but rather gave it what she wanted to give, that is, a meticulously researched, documented, articulated scholarly argument. She was no fool or envious child. She did not want to compete with Aldo, to take his beloved audience from him, but she did want to be honest and forthright and so she told the Captain and only the Captain of Aldo's cheating. The Captain had asked to see the 1928 catalogue not because he distrusted Constance but – he explained – because he needed verification before he could assert his authority. When Constance showed him the passages from the 1928 catalogue that Aldo had pasted together in his patchwork talk and that he never acknowledged, the Captain sat still as a stone. Staring off into space, he silently pulled at the hairs of his neat and trim mustache.

He instructed Constance to tell no one else. For the moment Aldo Brandini must be allowed to continue. He was, after all, the ship's most popular speaker and these were serious allegations. The difficulties of the times only compounded the seriousness of these allegations. Constance looked awry and the Captain asked her not to misunderstand him. He assured her that he would not let the crass economic concerns of the home office take precedence in this matter. Justice would prevail – all in due course.

But the next day no one spoke to Constance Wright and the looks she received! My God, Medusa could not match such stone producing venom. She cried alone in her cabin all that afternoon, but she resolved to attend Brandini's – the fiend! – evening lecture. She had so much pride.

She sat near the back of the hall and those who entered last took their chairs away from where Constance sat and isolated her like the bad child in class. When Brandini spoke – staring straight at her, smiling – she nearly fell off her chair. "When I see a beautiful building of exact order and proportion taken down," he began, "and the different materials laid together by themselves it puts me in mind of these commonplace men." At first she nearly screamed, then she almost started to cry again, but finally she resolved to bite her bottom lip which trembled uncontrollably and to sit there to the very end and thus deprive the great Brandini of some of his wicked pleasure.

When Brandini finished speaking, when the last slide flipped one notch further in its tray and the room momentarily went dark, the audience erupted in vociferous applause. Women screamed. Men chanted, made fists, and shook them in the air as they chanted. Aldo threw kisses to the women in the audience; some fainted. The noise became unbearable for Constance. The whole ship seemed to shake with shouting and the stamping of feet. She ran from the room clutching her pocketbook to her breast.

From up on the top deck she caught her first sight of land since they had left their last port of call. The noise, diminished by the decks, no longer drove her wild with fury and hate. Along the edge of the distant horizon she could discern the lofty markers of an ancient burial ground. Moments later or perhaps several hours later she saw pacing the shore a throng of bearded men, in sad-colored garments, and gray steeple-crowned hats, intermixed with women, some wearing hoods and others bareheaded.

No one argued with her, no one questioned her, no one replied to her in any way. In fact, no one said anything, at least not to her. Silence, she thought, must mean either consent or dissent – though she did not know which. She would not admit it, but her words were a soliloquy; her audience herself.

Inarticulate. All night she rambled, remembering more the sea than the infinitesimal mark of man upon it. What memories. Oddly, all that remains from that season at sea is the memory of wild flowers – once, at least, risky, but now the wildness tamed has become what? An offensive maneuver launched against the beaches of self. She wanted to forget both past and present, be done with it all, move along to her future, say to Saint Peter, "How do you do," and meet her maker. She had had enough.

She acted just like all the rest, a robot on the all day topside parade. Boxed in, trapped, her liberty forsaken for the sake of some no good godforsaken sea going social order. Well-wetted with drink, she became silly. For an instant she almost approached a reverential remembrance of the people of her troubled tour as well as the ship that contained them. The truth kept us apart. I will sink or swim in this world, she thought. Yet she could not forsake the memory: the people, not the ship. She'd once walked with a boyfriend down to the river and standing on a promontory her boyfriend only said "Gets Pretty Wide Here." The rest of the time they were silent. That was long ago. Sometimes at night she'd go by herself and build a campfire in a circle of blue-colored stones she had gathered from the shore. Tomboy, she'd watch the colors mingle and become lifelike. The sky met the earth at an angle along the railroad tracks' embankment. Who needed to speak? This was the silent place. Only breath sustains what words destroy. What is wrong will drown in language. I will sink or swim in the world, she thought.

Sunrise and time for her to meet the day. Simple. Simple work for a single day's time. It was all pre-arranged. She just had to eat, talk, smile, laugh, chuckle, grin, sign. She felt tempted to throw her quarter as hard as she could at the tollbooth attendant's eyes. Later, the Captain winked, smiled, shook her hand, said "Smooth sailing, Sailor!"

Later, she parked in the unpaved lot. She wore sunglasses. Not so much as a mask as a habit. She was a tourist. Here to see the late autumn foliage. The rows of pines strung out along the drives, the sun golden against the hills radiant with autumn colors. It wasn't here at the source, nor had it ever been. On land or sea she was a vegetable eating brontosaurus, extinct. She ran, desiring a gun to shoot at all the leaves on the all the trees. Careful aim, as a leaf falls she'd blow it to smithereens.

The knee-deep water was frigid. She waded out to skip rocks in the river, to look around; to figure something out. Blue-rocks along the shore. The sun was setting blood-red against the western sky. Campfire of blue-rocks gathered from the shore burned blood-red.

She watched. The beer kegs of prior times had become powder kegs somewhere out there in the dark black distance. But the slapping sound of tiny waves kept calling her Fool! Fool!

Two Plus Two

HE HAD A RED TIE he left hanging over the sink to dry. He was sure of it, a necessity for his job on the embankment, both his red tie and his sureness. Without it he'd be lost, unrecognizable among the others, profitless. He had checked all the cupboards, all the closets, all the drawers. Now he sat forlorn, lost in his own small room. He moved outside and checked around the stairs and the shrubs and the sidewalk and curb: still no red tie. Precious few minutes remained before he had to depart for his job on the embankment, but he could not go to work without his tie and he couldn't remain here either. There are no sick days for a man in his position. He decided to go, to risk appearing without his red tie, to explain the situation and hope for the best.

He found that as he neared someone, some anonymous passerby on the street he could not face that person, not that person or anyone else. He ducked behind the hedges, unkept and overgrown this time of year, as walkers in the city approached near enough to him to begin to get clear sight of him, but not so close that they could be sure that he had or he had not his red tie. He soon realized that his game of hide and seek took too long, that at this rate he'd be very late for his job on the embankment, very late for work. Brazenly, then, he stepped forward, chin up and chest out, and proceeded directly down the street, not meeting anyone's eyes but with full concentration setting himself in the direction of his destiny. He arrived without incident.

"Ah, so you knew. Had wind of it, I see," the dialogue maker said as he saw him approach tie-less.

"Had wind of what?" he wondered though he said nothing for he wasn't sure where this was going.

"Took courage to walk all this way like that," the dialogue maker said. "Perhaps that's why you've been selected. But how could you know; how could you have found out?"

"Sir, I know nothing."

"Well, you better know *something* soon, lad. Today is your promotion day. You've been selected to wear a new tie, a blue tie and a tie clasp, too."

"And a tie-clasp, too!"

"And a tie-clasp, too."

When he returned to his own small room that night he thought little of what had happened to him that day; he folded his new tie, his blue tie neatly and placed it gently in a drawer; he took his tie clasp and put it far, far away from the sink. Then he knelt by his bed, thanked God, climbed up and in, and went to sleep.

Entry

THERE IS NO MIDDLE to the story, only to the book. She is able to live in one or the other circle, but never in both and never in the middle. The same chemicals that produced raw film stock were also essential ingredients in gunpowder. The self-reliant man dumps toxic waste in his neighbor's yard. Ideology to Jefferson meant "the science of the mind." The palace may be a spectacle, but the ruins are a warning not to live in the palace. Snow there; then, three days later, snow here. A rose is not a rose by any other name. It is something else entirely. Instead of after dinner cigars and conversations about how to make money, you return to watching the game and have no conversations and no plans for making money. There is a disaster outside. If the dead are described as "dead as a doornail" and if the dead go to heaven, then there must be doornails in the arms of God. He who has never spoken cannot teach the silent man to speak. What you call a leap of faith I call suicide. We ain't dead yet – we're only off being pirates.

A Matter of Habit, A Dead Man

DEVOID OF ROMANTIC and gone the robbery which was not the entire period. The rationalization of fundamental need helps the individual. The basic conflict assumed is emotional. It becomes possible to classify, to synthesize experience. I assume that to understand the presence of the expected symbolism, it will do to analyze only its narrative structure and the resolution of conflicts. As society changes, a hero estranged from his society (in fact, he is the only character ever filmed alone against spectacular mountains), joins, leaves, enters, or abandons society.

There is a double miscalculation. Our families and our teachers will be shocked. Over us is blue sky. Hit in the eye, lads of eighteen.

By defeating the villains, as his last gesture shows, the society that threatens the hero is fought since the fight itself generates the values that replace the values of the society. Instead of marrying and settling down, specialists suggest that essentially they should act as individuals. Oppositions create images; a market economy, political legitimization. For the present, meaningful human relationships enjoy the benefits of freedom from incompatibility. To become autonomous, to eschew personal profit, to establish a market – we must identify "commitment." We have seen an aristocratic tendency with a democratic bias, but that is because of luck rather than determined effort. The hero can only be an individual when he is among others.

Those things that don't fit, madden. Ridiculous, assume its own truth; contribute to a better world. It is scientifically right! (Not so easy: plots, not myths for the unchanging mind.) To find an answer, motivated by error, what could be possible? The only way to understand the world is through the senses; therefore, pursue the most sensual experiences. Each a "special case." At its center spin faster, tighter. From its perimeter, convenience. We are complex swimmers.

Queue. Pithily. Palatial. Billets. Ostracized. Agitation. Emphatically. Obliterate. Renunciation. Discomfiture. *Esprit de corps.* Indignant. Lorry.

It started. A tired old town. Ladies bathed before noon. School's different. Now tell your father not to teach you anymore. Have a seat now. (Mortification.) I walked. By the time we reached their ways. I put ourselves in her shoes. And we were at all times free.

I spent. She had never. "You're the best." He ain't got a beard. Why, it did not seem *malignant.* (I can remember.) And wrenched it tight. And walk around in it. (Ascertaining.) It was that I had not heard him.

"Looks almost like he'd talk to you."

His eyebrows came together and he peered up at me. "Apoplectic." It was times like these ...

She was horrible. She would draw. After all those things, her weight. They've got to want to ...

You don't. Oddly. You know. Funny. I told you. That's what I thought. Hey, look. (Bullet-studded belt.)

Insatiable. Laconic. Insubordination. Benumb. Remnant. Suffice. Obliquely. Apparition. Dilate. Solace. Sultry. Malicious. Audible. Docile. Pallid. Tremulous. Plume.

Never ask. It gave him no pleasure. Then she thought, he was making fun of her. For some reason, I didn't go. We couldn't. But, what happened after that had a dreamlike quality.

That's what it is: a shadow. "I'll never understand," I said. I hadn't meant to be funny. (*Oppressed.*) The ladies were cool in fragile pastel prints. How sweet the sound. You know. That's all they did, the tribute. After that: furtive gait; his arm, off. (*Shoot.*) [ACQUIESCENCE]

Laudable. Importune. Opalescent. Obscure. Implacable. Extenuation. Fastidious. Surreptitiously. Fatuous. Proffer. Aberration. Emaciated. Insensate. Divinations.

Ascribe all honor. Even the manuscript seemed to be virtually quarrels and denials grown out of absence and criticism. The manuscript was engaged essentially to be the following initial execution within these three broad lines.

Origins

WE ARE DIRT beneath the product's feet. We will reply to James Fennimore Cooper – later. First: the Prologue. Pleasure as darkness shook his head. Our Lady wore the bridle and winnowed it in the wind. History sensed something I noticed and repaired to the house of his uncle, but our perceptions will put on vestments. As he stood there he took a clean map in the press, a clean sense of honor in the service. This enclosure could transfer memories as much as his own home. In his experience the rock shut within shells could hardly reach back so far.

The more they built – desire and dreams – both, the more the earth became warm. The things they value most are to kiss in agonized figures and the table at the fire warming to the blaze. And you, you cannot introduce the dark things: his swarthy body and all its blood, this mountain so heavy with cactus whips. Everybody laughed. A year from now I shall be given oracular significance at the bottom of a ditch.

One humble singer was entertaining the officers at the post, the natural beauties of his country, the solemn widow. In those days several trees waved feathery plumes of bluish green into blankets shut against her. Tremors passed; all that is past.

Only a woman could know the fervor always realized that distant missions surpassed. In his youth this was exactly it, any landscape or birds through the air. At a distance sat none of the shadows patience cast to improve unhurried flight. Within the last year the little towns all agreed to push these enterprises, as he still called them. Nobody embraced the vanished harvest, the moisture of bright edges, the leisure to write down "faster now." The bayonet seemed an injustice in isolated hearts, exhausted eyes.

Unblocked, we will have to see the face of this work. Perhaps it might be a little too comfortable, almost accidental. It becomes difficult for me to see out of it. It's so funny and I am a little sad. Isn't that odd. It is a kind of death. It becomes preposterous, waste, spots of gold, devils, a single sentence, Tuesday, a month ahead, accurate, unlikely, necessary, determined, frightened, immense.

But this was not necessary. He had already seen the ribbon. He arose from his seat feeling weak and slightly nauseated, his eyelids low against the black pupils. But that time a forgotten cigarette had possession of the loiterers so absorbed in the darkness. She also came down along the street where he would have an opportunity to join her at tea. But no, she cannot describe the men who had been injured and silent. She looked sleepy and she was staring with a strange fixedness at the deceptive atmosphere. When I think over this rumor, its gloom will emerge without that misery which should have interested or disturbed me. The wild ritual of work lies like demons around your family. Still, all frolics are regarded as barometers. Scrupulous accuracy, its chief merit.

Listening to the TV

IT WAS FEAR NO LONGER GOVERNED much less judged. The blood would remain an obviously necessary measure. A special world could not restrain its fruits and thus everything was done by marooned languages. That there would have been no nations tended to define the meaning of living in a relationship of the external sun. It was desire, a measure of self-respect.

There was very little (if any) change in an image so totally the reverse of what these years keep. Blame the emergence on the previous nation, a culmination of local reform efforts. A strange combination of the old and the new restored value to the one great barrier to other families. As merchants saw it, the problem was to collapse all institutions into a loosely rooted initiative for the construction of new subway routes. High cost deterioration, the absence of a thought has been countered by a way to become invisible. It was seen as the antithesis of a distorted and negative image. Politics proved a wedge, but political leadership would never improve.

By isolating one problem from the maze at least two misfortunes were owned and managed: a loss of respect for oneself and for life in general. Essentially, to achieve certain humane reforms government both could and should act to forestall breakdowns. The responsibility for a minimum subsistence is our own. Sharply divided, yet highly satisfactory and substantially adopted, the private self constituted nothing less than a passage of power and free rein to the sponsors of the message. Not until the inherited made matters worse, devaluing the dollar, was the paradox prevented from getting new mobilization.

Who was to blame? Virginians built a kind of stability out of instability. Freedom meant to be as free as possible. It is difficult to identify the first stirring of their image of themselves, their self-esteem, their conviction of their own superiority bringing freedom to the world: a means to an end.

Control the functions that can be manipulated one at a time. Without different operating systems, increase productivity and efficiency. As these are thoroughly and recklessly selfish in their endeavors, thoughtful men must surely be resolved of temper.

What event is this? I will never be purged away. I await the hour of my public murder. I am permitted to die for a cause. I cannot now, the scaffold has already.

In November, all these terrible calamities deemed it necessary to reflect upon the attitude so far inspired. Friends, the truest and strongest, hardly seemed such: vitality ground in mass dignity. But, in vivid contrast, the passive achievement central to the new ethos was silently ratified. A consensus marked out the permissible limits. The essential ingredient, finance, had shaken the very foundations. The excess allied with both old parties to restructure an uninformed kind of cultural pioneering. The essence was memory and shared personalities compelling the masses by allegiance to the cooperative crusade.

To escape the world did not fit with the description they had been taught since infancy to believe. From the Gulf to the Ohio River, fashion merged separate currents of energy. Social conformity for a variety of reasons, including pride, developed a new sense of mission. Deference was the crop. The Lamb had to swim upstream against the era patriotic – rigid plateau of mass loss and recipes from scratch.

Remove stem ends in large saucepan. Wash. Combine, tie legs together; cover all.

The Crossing

1 *No Accident*

SHE SENT ME her last drawing. It was a self-portrait completed in Paris before her death. She mailed it from somewhere within the Sixth Arrondissement at sometime during the morning of the fifth of May. There is so much that can be told from postage marks and there is so much that can't. I know nothing of her mood, her thoughts, what dress she wore on that final morning. Was it the one we bought together at Bergdorf's in New York before she left? Was it that one? I am reminded of how difficult it was to remove all the manufacturer's tags when we got it home that day and she was about to try it on once more but the staples and the thread and the instructions for care slowed her down. "The instructions for care": I am reminded of all of this, and much more than just this as I sit here at my desk and try to think of how best to explain this to her children. The pens in their holder stare at me, the books on the shelf stare at me, the stapler stares at me, the tape stares at me – every possession stares at me, accuses me, calls me guilty, says I did not read too carefully the instructions for care.

How will I tell her children? What can I write to them? They never liked me and the woman they knew is not, was not the woman I knew. Why do we refer to what remains as the body, the corpse; never the person and never by the person's name? The polite officer called this morning. He told me they found the body under the bridge. He spoke excellent English. I speak little French. He told me they found the body and I spun the postcard by its corners on my desk as he spoke. It was the postcard of the week before. We seldom used phones. It was about rain though sun shone brilliant over the

Cathedral. It was about silence though every millimeter was full. It pictures that bridge, that one beneath which they found the body. Should I tell her children about the body, about the rain, about the silence?

The officer said that there is no question about it. No accident, he said. There are witnesses. (Can I have their names?) There will be no investigation. I can claim the body at the airport in no more than three days. Maybe sooner. I can make all the arrangements. He said I should get started right away. I should get started right away because she will be home soon. He must be a sentimentalist. He, too, is averse to the formal phrase: "the body." He is very much like me then. Will he use her name before he signs off?

I will tell her children that I have spoken to an official who guarantees that she is at Orly, that soon she will arrive at Kennedy. There is one thing I must add. I'll say to them that when she arrives, if you could be there to greet her, I'll say, you would not recognize her. The woman they knew is not the woman I knew. They live somewhere out there in a timeless nowhere, the past; I live here. I am responsible.

The phone rings again. It is the airlines informing me that the flight has been delayed, that they don't know when the plane will take-off, that they don't know when the plane will land, that they can't even be sure that it'll still land at Kennedy. Perhaps Baltimore, he says. Then he assures me, don't worry your wife is fine.

I hang up the phone, I go over to the chair by the door, lift my raincoat from the chair, walk to the closet further down the front hall, go to the closet, open it, turn on the light, hang the coat up. Then I turn off the light and close the door and I walk to the living room and sit-down in a chair there next to the piano. I stare at the photographs. I wait for the phone. I wait for the children. It is dark and silent with the lights out. It is dark in my heart and I cannot gather sufficient will to call them, those who already dislike me so.

I avoid the issue, the responsibility. I will go to the airport and wait, for six or seven hours – minimum – I will wait. In the airport there is so much to do. There is a donut shop, a store that sells products made in New York state – cheddar cheese made by up-state Amishmen, for example. This cheese has travelled to Tanzania, has travelled to Ohio. There in the airport, there in the airport there is a sufficient supply of paper to write to everyone. They will know soon enough. I will go and wait.

There is a fork in the road. One direction leads to the airport; one direction leads to the beach. Which would you choose, if you had to choose? Here are the waves of the Sound quietly waving goodbye one by one, one for everyone. Why write? We've already arrived.

He lifts one leg out of the water, stands like an ancient God, and watches the planes circle in their endless patterns overhead. He realizes then what word the patterns spell, he realizes she has landed and that his wife is fine.

I thought that the third person end with its romanticized death just wouldn't do. I put the pen down. I put the paper away in the drawer. I got that coat back out of the closet and went out to tell them all the truth.

2 *Echoes*

"Imagine how frightening it would be to see yourself. I mean to really see yourself. You're sitting in your comfy chair and you look across the street and there in the window you see yourself looking back at you. Really you. It would be frightening for anyone. You'd probably die of fright. One of you anyway." He paused then and seemed to count to three before continuing.

" 'If you average all the hills and all the valleys of the world, what do you get? Sea level.' That's what I said. That was my discovery. You see: for every up hill there is an equal and opposite down hill.

You may not find it when you want to find it, but it's there alright," he said at least for that moment satisfied and content.

"Believe me. What I'm telling you is absolutely true because I've been everywhere and seen everything." This he said with great emphasis, as if a verdict hung on it. "You know," he added, "I was on the Missouri with MacArthur in Tokyo Bay."

"No, I didn't know that." Was his reply just a touch sarcastic? If it was, the older man did not sense it or if he did, he ignored the younger man's slight and continued nonetheless.

"And I've been to all the cities, all the major cities. Budapest, Berlin, Basra – not just the Bs either. Every letter. All twenty-nine."

"There aren't that many." The younger man did not look at the older man. He looked straight ahead; he looked at nothing in particular. He spoke as if by rote.

"There are more than you can imagine. Once in Istanbul the four of us …" he spoke now with growing excitement, "went to the market and had a fight with one of the vendors. Short guy, but tough. And his whole family had knives. Naturally, we just had the use of our hands and our brains. You have to say that for the 101st."

An interruption: "Yes, you have to say that." And a road block: "And where did you say you were from?"

"Well, at the moment, Paris, but I still tend to think of Parsippany as home." He smiled then. "Another one of the great P cities, you might say."

"You might. But not to be mistaken with P town. Right?" Did he smile, too, then?

"Right."

"Could you pass the nuts."

"You know that was what Clark said. He had balls."

"You couldn't have been there, too." He was incredulous.

"Europe, Japan, Africa. I saw every theater of action. Special Operations, you know." He wore a somewhat wrinkled suit, not pressed fatigues, but seemed to look in the general direction of his shoulder as he spoke the words "Special Operations."

"And Paris?"

"Business." His head bent now a bit, not so peacock proud as moments before. The younger man had been touched.

"How long do you think we'll wait?"

"Well, it's hard to say with these smaller companies."

"Must be a cheap company you work for." He felt bad that he had said this, but, he figured, it was too late now.

"The cheapest." Indeed, yes, there was a bitterness.

"No Air France? No American?" He tried to lighten the mood.

"No. Just these charters." Pause, and a moment, just a moment of quiet. "Can I get you another drink?"

"Might as well." He said, his mood lightening. "It doesn't look like we're going anywhere."

"What'll you have?"

"Just a beer," a quick, automatic reply, but he followed this with: "s'il vous plaît" and he smiled then.

"Yeah, right." The older man, on the other hand, did not smile.

"What's in the bag?" The younger man asked.

"Clothes," he said. "Gave up with suitcases. If I can carry everything on, then I get off quicker. Once I went from Paris to New York to Bradley – the Hartford airport, to O'Hare to L.A. then to Rome and back to Paris, all with one sport coat rolled up in a bag." He seemed proud, boastful, nostalgic. He waved his hand in the air as if to say "just so," as if to say "I am a magician."

The younger man felt that he had pierced the mysteries, but appearances can be deceiving and the hand is quicker than the eye and so on. He said with some emphasis, some confidence and certainty, "Maybe if you wore a pressed suit, looked professional, they'd put you on another, on major airlines."

"No way." One could almost hear behind these words the word "idiot" echo even though left unsaid. "You see, it's a family run company and a very cheap family at that. Believe it or not, I'm Executive Vice-President for European Distribution."

"Distribution?" The light bulb lit again. "Does that mean it's a film company?"

"Paramax. I've been with them since the war."

"You've lasted that long!" Appearances can be deceiving, etc.

"Sorry, I mean my preconception is that everyone's career in entertainment is either short lived or always changing."

"True." Interested now. "For the most part. There are some of us, though, who've had a certain longevity."

His turn: "Can I get you another drink?"

"What?" An interruption, a road block. "Oh, yeah. Sure. Martini, dry."

And then a detour: "Never could drink them myself. Just beer or wine for me. Belgium beer I think is the best. Even better than British."

So much for any recitation of the truth, he thought. "That's the trouble with you young people. There's something soft about you." He looked him over. "Soft and international, but at the same time provincial. The effect of the Internet, I suppose. You think you have access to the world, but fail to realize they've made the whole world one big company town." Satisfied.

"Who has?" Confused.

"Paramax – all the others in collusion with one another." Certain.

"That's a rather dim view of things, isn't it?" Offended now and ready to defend his generation with sarcasm. He wasn't quite sharp enough for irony. Not today. "Is that another of your discoveries?"

"No. I think that's the truth." His parental tone quickly shifted to something more philosophical, if not prophetic. "It's right in front of everybody's nose, but because it's so close, few see it." And then the nostalgia, disappointment, and despair returned. "As for my discoveries ... I've been saying those same stupid lines since prep school."

"Time for a new act?" For some reason despite the older man's self-reproach, he wasn't sympathetic at all.

"Too late." And then that old, tired, worn stare into the empty glass.

"Why don't you retire?" There was, yes there was a *bubbly* tone to the young man's voice.

"Why don't you take a long walk off a short pier." That seemed to say it all.

"Prep school?"

"Princeton Country Day."

"And family?"

"Paramax."

"That's kind of sad."

"Sad, no; true, yes."

"And they put you on charter flights?"

"And they put me on charter flights."

He got up to go to the men's room. "Pee," he said and nothing more. The younger man held a book and looked into it deeply, deeply as if it were a mirror.

3 *Beatrice*

It makes absolutely no sense. I don't know if it will comfort you or make you feel worse. It's mysterious. I don't know. And I've never told anyone. Jim knows – sort of, because I wrote a story about it. Sort of. But I destroyed it later. Even erased it from the computer. That far. Every time I hear that music I think of her only because I associate the music with her. That's what I was listening to on the train. Just as easily I could associate the music with Paris – everyone was listening to it – but I don't.

Yes, I would have kicked everything. I took two days off and if she had just said the word, any word – you know what I mean? I would have never showed up again. Off to, to Tanzania. Like that, just like that. The attraction – for me – was immediate and so overwhelming. So, what's the use of falling, of falling in love, as the song says. Don't. It's safer not to. What do you do with the knowledge? Where store it? How understand it? Is this any help or does it just piss you off? Let me know.

I'm so lucky to have had so few real disappointments. I mean you just can't sit and write only after you've had too much to drink, can you? Discipline, discipline, discipline and a good pen, though I guess that reveals my age or something. Still, a pen.

How could it be? You've got to excuse me. It's been a long day and it's not going to get any shorter. I'm not doing what I'm supposed to be doing and I look over there and see that book by the newsstand and wonder, but also understand. What writing! She deserves it. Good luck. What am I to do?

I meant to tell you a little story as a way to comfort you, my good friend. The wait is too long; the feeling, too unusual, bizarre, abstract. I miss her when I hear that music even though it makes no sense. Foolishness. Childishness. This can't make it any easier for you. You'll now have even less faith in your fellow *man*, right? What's the point? No delay, no confession. But here we are. Does any of this make any sense?

No. And don't try to put words in my mouth. There's absolutely no reason for you to have told me this, any of it. Why do you persist in your fraternities even as grown men? Did you think your words would exonerate him? Who is the story therapeutic for in this instance? You disappoint me. The least you can do is order another glass of wine, compliment my hair. Excuse yourself and get on out of here. You? You, too?

"Is there somewhere we can go? There's something I have to ask you."

"Why? I don't see the point of it."

"There's something I have to know."

And if he saw her, would she tell him? And if she told him, would it matter to either of them?

I am reading about memory now. There is no place in which the past gets stored. Memory is nothing more than a random set of electrons and all recall works by way of association in the present. In other words, there is no such thing as recall. I used the wrong word. Nothing remains. What seems to be prior event is a construction of random impulses in the present, though people shape these impulses to fit their present needs. This is psychoanalysis; self-analysis. What is it that I need? Is it you?

No, it's not me. You don't know me. The heart of another is a dark forest always. What would happen if I were to walk in here right now? What if right before take-off I was the last to board? If I sat next to you?

You see, his first love moved away when they were young and he never got over it and so he seems to wander the earth looking for her though much of the year he lives out of his van on Key West. She is his Beatrice.

She does not recall his name. She lives in Tucson and is the mother of five. She teaches Sociology at Norwich University in Vermont, lives alone, and hates the young women who take the military track, but says nothing. It's just a job. She died in an automobile accident near her home outside of Philadelphia during her sophomore year as a commuter student at Rosemont College. She is a nurse in a neo-natal care unit at a large urban hospital. She is a legislative analyst in a large northeastern state. She is a songwriter. She is the author of that book by the cash register. She cannot recall his name. She recalls other things because she has different needs.

As she sits, waits, converses, she knows what she's talking about with anyone who stops for an autograph or pauses just long enough to say hello, to nod – at least – in recognition. She knows the shape of the carrot in her eye. The money in her pocket burns a hole in her heart through which the wind and rain blows and her heart, it falls out upon the floor through this hole. I can see this because once long ago I knew her or are some electrons just flying about, heating up my brain, scrambling the network? She carries all her belongings with her in a scarf tied with string. No one recognizes her. I touch her hand. What can one expect, after all? I whisper her name. Once she travelled across the bridge at her doorstep and returned with nothing more, nothing less. Once she looked inside her scarf and her beating red heart surprised her. "There you are," she said, letting a cat play with the string now abandoned at her feet, but not with her heart. No, not with her heart. That she held close and tight. The carrot remained in her eye, a sight she'd long ago set her eye on that grew bigger all the time. Now that she could hold her heart in her hands, close and tight, she had her carrot, too. She put her heart aside and held the carrot up high and used it to beat the wind and the rain. She told me so herself while, just by chance, we waited, years later, for the very same plane.

4 *Rights of Man*

He sees only the bright color of the plane, not its stillness; not its red upholstered emptiness. The first thing you'll see is the gilded wood framed mirror encircled with rose petal stenciling. You'll be struck by the rich fragrance of lavender as your eye averts to the sparkle of the jewelled elephant. This is a special treasure; the prize of the collection. It came from Tanzania several centuries ago. Once it belonged to tribal kings who waged war for it more than once so prized a possession was it. Then there is the tray, a simple beige ceramic tray of deco design used to hold hair pins and other cheap decorative ornaments for the body. The juxtaposition will not be alarming; the Belgian lace doily beneath the tray, expected.

Look up above the tray to the lower right hand of the mirror and you'll see a postcard from Paris wedged into the mirror's frame.

The color of the cafe umbrellas matches that of the rose petals. Beyond the cafes and their umbrellas one can see a bridge. Nothing else is stuck into the frame of the mirror. Nothing else is in the view on the postcard. The mirror's edge is not crowded with memos or mementos, just a postcard from Paris that pictures cafes, umbrellas, and, in the distance beyond, a bridge. There are no people. No cigarettes.

In the assemblage atop the dresser the absence of people in the postcard is rectified by a photograph of the entire family. The photograph shows one of those holiday occasions with all present. Even the photographer himself is in the picture. Timer set. Ready. Go. There are fourteen people in this image; there is no need to describe here each individual face. That's another story. Call it: "No Cigarettes" – if you like. I was the photographer who gathered everyone together, got them to behave, set the timer, ran around to the back of the group, outstretched my arms to tighten the group as best I could, and said, "Say pizza!" just as the shutter opened and clicked; the flash, flashed. What a good picture it turned out to be. Lucky. Anywhere USA. It is in an imitation gold drugstore frame.

You see, all the surrounding bric-a-brac disguises the costliness of that antique, bejewelled elephant. Yet, who's to say that to its owner the object d'art is so valued? Or, even that its value is known and recognized? Perhaps it's like that just discovered Michelangelo that was there all along in a courtyard fountain, there for a century and the owners thought it no more than worthless kitsch. Perhaps its the image of the fourteen framed faces that's most prized, their lips all slightly parted in just the same way – the result of beginning to blissfully shout out the word "pizza" but having had the shutter close before they reached the "a" of that word, "pizza." No one knows what's what or to whom. Or only one knows. Not me. Is it the elephant, the photograph, the postcard, the tray or the objects upon it? Perhaps something else. She would know. Perhaps the perfume. Yes, it is the perfume brought back from Union Square in San Francisco. The saleswoman would spray one, look up toward the ceiling, inhale, look away, spray another in another direction, and repeat the procedure. Over and over again she did this. I could not tell them apart, but I caught on that it was something like a wine tasting (I had been north of the city in Sonoma County the day before) and one clears the nose with air between sniffs as one cleans the palate with water between sips. She said that she preferred one particular costly scent for day and another even costlier one for the night and so I took both that she had recommended. She complimented me, my largesse. What a guy. The Count of Pittsburgh. I shall wear a patch across one eye and a cape upon my back.

What else is there: a little plastic monkey from the amusements at Fisherman's Wharf (a different trip – together that time), an elaborate cloth covered box containing more hair pins and ties, a bright yellow pin cushion (no pins in it for the Countess does not sew) with four bumble bees protruding from its sides struggling to hold on, and a tape measure in the shape of a little green house. There's always something to measure: the day; the globe. The wait.

Should I mention what's inside? The top drawer, the middle drawer, the bottom drawer? I'll devote a paragraph to each and then end with the mirror again, rather poetically noting that your face enters the mirror as you enter the room. But first, the top drawer. This is the special one, a fetish for every Count throughout the land, the one of delicate things belonging to the Countess. How did Mrs. Danvers put it in *Rebecca*: "lace underwear woven by French nuns"? Well, yours are of the store bought variety but nonetheless may still be romanticized, eroticized. Let's leave the rest to the imagination.

In the second drawer there are tee shirts. This is America. In the third drawer there are hats and gloves. Some are yours; some are mine. I'm brief here because I'm getting tired of thinking about this, getting tired of waiting, getting tired of all these cigarettes. All this thought uses up surprisingly few minutes. Let's sell the elephant and get better flights. This sucks. All this smoke. Sell the elephant.

Sell the elephant. There is no elephant just hair ties and doilies and baskets and trays and a plastic monkey and a postcard of certain completely deserted streets, etc.

"There can be no such thing as a nation flourishing alone in commerce; she can only participate; and the destruction of it in any part must necessarily affect all. When, therefore, governments are at war, the attack is made upon the common stock of commerce, and the consequence is the same as if each had attacked his own."

In other words, both suffer. Your face enters the mirror as you enter the room. Oh, Penelope: "when the tongue or the pen is let loose in a frenzy of passion, it is the man, and not the subject, that becomes exhausted."

5 Motown

I want to react to what I'm reading without all this knowledge. There comes a point when knowledge becomes a kind of pollution that blocks a more honest vision, a clearer sight of the object itself. I hate waiting in these damn airports. Patience was never a strong point with me. Say a word, at least: "sorry" or something. I can't read anymore *the thing itself*. All is a mesh of movable screens. Here we sit, blinded by what we know which inhibits our will to act. The song repeats, over and over again.

My love. I haven't seen him in over six months and here I am in this God forsaken hell-hole, Orly Sud, what a name, while he is waiting at home wondering if I'm alright. I may be dead for all he knows. This isn't fair. Or maybe he's so busy doing what it is he's doing that he hasn't even noted the time. So into his work that it's a kind of pollution that blocks his vision of the actual hour, the clock set right before him or the wristwatch on his wrist; the beat of his heart: tick-tock. Rock around the clock.

I feel anxious and silly, sitting here alone waiting for my

homebound flight. Someone nearby watches a *Gilligan's Island* re-run on a coin operated TV. It is dubbed in French. Gilligan sounds so sweet, but the Captain, he is ridiculous in French and I am tired of French. I am tired of people who won't speak English even if they know the language, even if you ask very politely in their own language for them to speak a bit in yours. All of this is a wall, a wail. He's dead. I'm dead. Bang, bang. You're dead. Over and over again. There's nothing to do. There's nothing to do.

The agony of waiting to see the one that you love: this is a theme that they should understand, that should be close to their romantic nature and should hurry them along. "Now boarding," the cry goes out and we greet it with relief. Shouldn't it? Unless they're dead, dead to it. I want to go home. Simple as that, really. I feel like a bird perched on a tree, a little tiny fake tree inside a cage. Rocking Robin. Tweet, tweet. And I thought that I was on a roll of good fortune, lucky. Picked first by a prize patrol. There is no need for this wait-ing, this pollution of purpose and understanding. I do not know what is happening and no one says anything. Am I dead? It is 12:01, a new day here; dinner time there. Will he see the hour now? Is he moved from his concentration by the rumble in his stomach? Off to a pizza party with lab partners perhaps? Sing song, let's move along. Get going. Louisiana Hayride. Move along now. How much longer must I wait? It is 12:01. That man seated at the bar, that fa-miliar looking man has gotten off his barstool, his high stool, his high horse, high school. He strolls; I sulk. Shit. How much longer must I wait.

Somethings come out OK and others don't, yes? I am totally con-fused. No question mark there. No raised inflection of the voice. This wouldn't be happening if I flew Delta instead of this damn charter. My underwear and bra are too tight. All these hours, a bar-rette tight in my hair. I feel as if I'll pass out from boredom if this plane does not board soon. My clothes choke me. The television maddens me. The smiling men in the bar disgust me. I can't wait to hear English spoken again. I was wrong, even Gilligan sounds awful in French. He is not the Gilligan that I know. That familiar looking man at the bar: I do not know him. I am sure of that. I hate him. I am sure of it. God has left the world as it is now. Timelessness. Here I sit. Forever. Purgatory. Hell. Damnation. Charter flights. Pollution.

Oᴋ. I'll change my attitude. Think positive. This is good. I need to learn patience. To see through all this pollution and filth. Patience is a quality that I lack. Alright people, let's wait! Then again, patience only stretches so far. Let's end it right here. Get my last will and testament out and read it. Divide up all my prizes and my prize possessions. All my books and bows and hair ties, too. Let's end it here. Where is your lawyer when you need her? Where is the Wizard when you need him? I click my high heels but nothing happens. Just more noise in this din, in this den of obnoxious noise; just more pollution. Here I sit with these people that I don't even know and their loud, annoying laughter, Gilligan and clanging glasses in the background, a song over and over again in my head, this book in my hands and my inability to read it on its own terms. There is a point when knowledge becomes a kind of pollution that acts like a blow to the head, that keeps you passive or bang, bang you're dead. I knew very well that I'd save money, but lose time. Not this much, though. I couldn't have imagined that. This. Why didn't I go to some Carnival Del Soul in some languid Spanish town. Paris, always Paris. "We'll always have Paris." So why didn't I come back some other time? A bargain. A fool's bargain. Fool's gold, charter flights. "I'd walk a mile for a Camel." And smoke everywhere. More pollution. More ugliness. That man at the bar from before. A pig. My feet hurt and my back aches and all I want to do is get home, to see the one I love, to act again, not to sit so passive, not to complain so much, but to clear away all the pollution instead and to know once again your pure, sweet name. Let's hear it. The rest is blank. The rest is black. I will focus on this emptiness; this darkness: clip it, tie it, send it off, call it, too, something. Control it by calling it what I will call it. Use italics. Find a title even: *Green*. Then cut it back. Cut it off. Play a game. I'll say a word and you say the first word that comes to mind. "Lipstick" I say and you say "red." "Aluminum foil" I say and you say "food." "Documentary" I say and you say "film." "Cross" I say and you say "bear." Oh, I see, but I haven't got a chance. Not until I am awake in my life and out of here. Not until I can see water as well as think of words, words, words. Not until I'm back in his arms again. Baby, baby, baby: back in his arms again.

6 *Taxonomy*

"It was not easy to come to a consensus about what this bird was doing in the water. No one recognized it and a few said that they could not even see it. A strange looking bird, but this was a strange ship. Isabelle enjoyed it. It was her idea. A cruise ship where the only entertainment was a nightly lecture. Not too much ship board excitement there, but Isabelle enjoyed it. It was her idea, after all. Odd ship, really. All lectures and a peculiar looking bird in the water alongside, a bird that even the ship's resident ornithologist couldn't classify. Resident ornithologist. How many cruise ships have a resident ornithologist? Resident dance instructors, resident bridge players, yes, but an ornithologist? Great food, though."

"Well, it is remarkable, Henry, how much weight you've lost. How did you avoid over eating on a ship with nothing to do, but eat? How did you remain slim, keep the pounds off?"

"I didn't worry about it. Binge eating. Ate like a pig. Like I used to when you knew me so well. When we ate our way across five countries. We were only on board for a week or so and I knew it wouldn't make any difference. Starved myself when we got off in the Canaries. Starved myself in La Laguna despite the freshness of the fish."

"And then where from there?"

"We came up through Spain and got here about a week ago. It's easy to avoid over eating in Paris. Everyone's been here before, had their fill of it here and it seems everything is a gooy, rich sauce without the meat or as common as a pizza."

"It looks like we might be here for another week, too."

"I doubt it. We'll be off soon or else they would have offered to put us up at a nearby hotel." Henry paused a moment and then added, "The Airport Sheraton probably. Thinking to please us that way."

"Meet desires and destinations half-way, you mean?"

"Yes, if not to America, at least to an American hotel. No hotel. No extraordinary delay. You see how it goes, Matt? I'm sure of it. We'll be off soon."

"Listen to him. The expert of international flight. The sultan of airline service. If Henry says we'll be off soon believe me, Matt, we won't be off till noon the next day. Hotel or no hotel," Isabelle said.

She had arrived just that instant with four coffees well balanced in a cardboard cup caddie. She extended the caddie first to Matt, then to Henry, and last, after nearly turning around, she moved the caddie toward Kenneth. As she sat down with her cup, still in the caddie and surrounded by sugar packets and napkins, she said, "Well, Henry. Aren't you going to say hello to Kenneth?"

Henry looked dumbfounded for a moment. Then stood with his steaming cup in his left hand and extended his right hand to Kenneth.

As they shook hands, Kenneth said he envied how good Henry looked. "Slim as ever," Kenneth said. This comment took Matt a bit by surprise and he squinched up his eyebrows as if to say who is this stranger from Henry's distant past? Either he's a bit daft, a bit patronizing, or he just doesn't remember his old friend so well. For no one was ever as fat as Henry was fat. Indeed, one of their mutual friends, a poet in New York, had written a short piece about it that *The New Yorker* printed. About how this incredibly fat man would get into a taxi and the whole cab would sink down to the ground. That heavy. Such was Henry. Hence, "slim as ever" seemed the most preposterous thing possible to have said to Henry. Could it have been a joke? Matt wondered. No, there was no irony in his voice when he said it. It seemed that this Kenneth fellow honestly meant it!

Henry undertook the formalities of introductions while Isabelle maneuvered the coffee caddie on her knees and fumbled with sugar packets and napkins. She brushed off the plastic lid with a light motion of an extended napkin before removing it and emptying sugar into the cup. Henry, disapprovingly, watched this from the corner of his eye as he said: "Matt, this is my very dear, very old – old as in longtime not old as in years – my very *good* friend Kenneth Pimple. And Kenneth, this is my friend of more recent times, though he is to us as the sweetest Beaujolais Nouveau is to our host country, Matt Burns."

"Don't forget that middle initial," Kenneth said to Henry as he shook Matt's hand. "Boy, I used to get it in high school for that."

"That's right," Henry said. "It's not just Kenneth Pimple. It's Kenneth D. Pimple. ' Kenneth T H E Pimple,' everyone used to say. How could I have forgotten. And wouldn't you know that a guy cursed with a name like that would be the handsomest guy around. Got all the girls. Girls used to … "

But before Henry could finish Kenneth interrupted and after quickly glancing over at Isabelle told Matt rather quietly that Henry did OK himself in that regard. "Always so slim and trim," he said. "Svelte might be the word," he added. "Svelte, suave, and urbane. That was Henry. And so, too, he remains."

There it was again, Matt thought. Could they have known two different people who metamorphosed somehow into the single entity seated here with both of them today?

"Unlike me, Henry, you're handsome still, not tattered by these hostile years. I can see that quite clearly with my own two eyes. Here's the prooftext, the prooftext seated, situated, contextualized, and read as plainly as any open book," Kenneth rhapsodized. "Some things, some people never change. Thank God. They're our foundation, our bedrock, our anchor."

Isabelle chimed in just then: "I rather think of Henry as a ship that's sunk."

"And I," Matt said with rhetorical emphasis and flourish meant to match Kenneth's oratory, "and I think of Henry as buried treasure that's been found, that's surfaced once again."

"A bag of bones to the surface, so to speak?" Isabelle asked.

But before Matt could reply, before he could come to Henry's defense, if not his rescue, Henry himself spoke. "And me?" Henry implored mock-heroically. "Well, I've just got to be me." His words ended in the lilting phrase of song.

"Well that may very well be, Henry," Matt said. Since Henry had successfully deflected Isabelle's thrust, Matt turned his thoughts and attention back to the strange, incomprehensible words that Kenneth had spoken. "But Kenneth," Matt became quite serious, "I must tell you about the radical transformation that has occurred to Henry lately."

"He looks like he's still nineteen to me. You're very lucky, Isabelle." Kenneth turned toward her as he said this and Isabelle turned toward Henry as she said in a flat, unappreciative automaton's voice, "Yes, as Matt said, Henry is a treasure." Neither Matt nor Kenneth knew what to make of this. Henry smiled, that same old smile he had always smiled for years and years now, that smile that never changed even if the body or the heart it held did.

7 *The Place Where Money and Many Presents Were Given*

Most people would believe that she was much too old for such bright red clothes. She did not feel this way. Red remained her favorite color and her skirts remained remarkably short – even at her age. She thought she never looked better, that she got better looking every day. It is true that her red skirts seemed to get shorter every year, her red sweaters tighter, her red lipstick brighter, and her boyfriends younger. Her present companion was a slim, athletic young man of average height and twenty-two years of age. He was meticulously clean shaven, but a bit haphazardly dressed in ruffled blue jeans and a worn, gray v-neck sweater. He turned just then and lit the older woman's cigarette, a scene out of some out-of-date film, and she, in turn and just as scripted it seems, blew out the match, her lips pursed far to one side. It was all very stylized, if not choreographed. She sat with her legs crossed, left over right, her left hand on her left knee, her left sharply heeled black shoe half off and bobbing as she rhythmically shook her lower left leg. Impatient, it seems. The cigarette she held in her right hand and only occasionally did she put it to her glossed lips.

They had met sometime before, but not too long before, during another wait for another plane in another airport. She had worn bright red that day, too, though perhaps not quite so bright as the red she wore on this day. He had worn his jeans, perhaps the same pair; perhaps his only pair. And he had a coat, one of those knock-off raincoats made to look like the real thing yet somehow, at least to the woman in red, announcing itself as an inexpensive imitation. He seemed irritated that the only empty seat in the crowded waiting area was next to a woman who blew gusts of smoke from her rouged rimmed mouth and who smoked non-stop (non-stop, that is, the opposite of his intended flight). But his standing and shifting from foot to foot eventually wore him down and he then sat down next to her. She smiled and then exhaled in his direction.

He, politely, made no gesture at all, remained stone faced and steadfastly tired. When he awoke he realized he had rested his head on the soft material of this woman's red sweater, on the still sweet slope of her shoulder. More than tobacco he inhaled a very pleasant perfume as he moved his head away from her and apologized. She smiled and said something too softly for him to hear and he politely, he thought, did not ask her to repeat what she had said, but just quite simply smiled then.

He asked her if she would save his seat and watch his coat for him for a few minutes and she said yes – he heard her this time – and he went to the men's room then and when he returned he thanked her for watching his coat and saving his seat and she said yes, again, just "yes." He thought to himself that this woman might be old enough to be his mother, but he also thought that he was old enough to be her lover. He could be the lover of this woman who wears red and says yes. And so it came to pass. He became her lover, but she did not become his mother. For she was not caring and comforting, rather at times she was abusive and demanding. She did buy him a new coat, an original rather than an imitation. And he did grow used to the smoke while at the same time she learned to just dangle her cigarette, not to suck the smoke in deeply and blow it out profusely as she had done for many years. In fact, now she would only occasionally put the cigarette to her lips. She had thought of quitting, but hadn't, not yet; hadn't even mentioned it to him. Just in case.

There were plenty of other seats in the waiting area this night, but he gladly sat next to this woman old enough to be his mother with clothes on that anyone would think too youthful, too short, too tight, too red for her years. They sat there together and he moved his right hand to her left hand and clasped it there on the beautiful black stocking of her bobbing bony knee.

Soon he was asleep, again: asleep and content, just like the other time. In his dream he had a conversation with a friend of his back home, back where they were headed, back somewhere west of New York, and this is what he said to his friend in his dream as he rested boyishly waiting for a plane: "Oh, no. It's not like that at all. Maybe only once and that was more of a feeling than an action of any kind. Just a sense of being overwhelmed by love. Holding hands while watching *Citizen Kane* and there was a new scene in the film something about warm cakes and coffee and at first there was a hesitancy about holding hands, a fear, almost, because of rules and a certain desired respectability, but then, after awhile, a sense that the image of us holding hands could be telegraphed to the entire world. Please, yes, do so: tell the world. We're in love! And then I pulled her closer. And that's it. That and that incredible sense of peace."

8 *Guarantees*

"John, it says here that the best large model fan is the Beverly Hills Stratos 4605." Jimmy reported this information conscientiously, but John did not reply and so Jimmy tried another product.

"John," he said, "it says here the best two slice toaster is the Oster 3826," but John did not respond at all, not so much as a grunt, nod, or blink. Nothing, nothing at all.

And so Jimmy tried a full scale barrage of product information. "John," he began once more with his name, no model number, "it says here that the Mr. Coffee Accel PR12A is the best basic model automatic drip coffee maker and that the Cuisinart Little Pro Plus is the best compact model food processor. If you'd like a full-sized model then they recommend the Braun Multipractic VK11. Full-sized or compact, John? Full-sized or compact? Steam irons then or low flow toilets or big ticket items like cars, TVs, and stereos? Do they still use that word, John? Do they still say 'stereo'? I know, John. I'll check the index. Maybe it'll say 'stereo, see CD Player.' Boy, have times changed, John. The Black & Decker BV 1000 Handheld Electric Power Blower is the best. I would have thought Black & Decker would be at the top more often, John. I would have thought that, considering their reputation for quality, quality at a reasonable price. That's what I've always liked about Black & Decker. Quality at a reasonable price. That and availability. Can't find a town anywhere where you can't get your hands on a reasonably priced, smooth operating Black & Decker BV 1000 Handheld Electric Power Blower, John. Can't. Just can't."

John made an effort to speak suddenly and then just as suddenly fell back into his seat. He was despondent. Then he made a good, solid second effort, one-hundred and one percent moved those plaster lips and said, "Try to find one in Paris." He then fell back into motionlessness and silence and that glazed look in his eyes from having sat there for several hours watching the images on the little TV set screwed into a metal arm attached to his waiting room seat. There was no indication of manufacturer on it, just a white box of steel or a plastic hard as steel with various prints on places where others had pushed it left or right, up or down to adjust it for their viewing. He did not have any sound. He had Jimmy for sound and all the constant ambient noise that reached him from every direction. On the TV silent French reporters interviewed members of the audience of a French production of *Much Ado About Nothing* staged at the little theater below I. M. Pei's pyramid at The Louvre. John sat and watched; barely interested, unimpressed by the location, by the audience's gaiety, unmoved and seemingly unmovable, too, yet in someway envious.

"Jimmy," John said.

"Yes, John," Jimmy said.

"Why can't I be one of those people they interview? One of those people who they ask about the play, about the tax structure, about the verdict, about the war or the weather or whatever? How come it's never happened to me?"

Perhaps it was fate or maybe some kind of miracle even, but at precisely that moment, just as Jimmy was about to reply, just as he was about to say one thing, a French television crew went right by them, chasing after Jeanne Moreau, asking her a thousand questions, shinning bright lights at her. The reporter with the microphone in hand walked backwards, but turned partly every so often to make sure that he would not trip, fall, embarrass himself before the eyes of this national treasure, this shrine and her live audience of millions. He almost knocked into the television that John watched. Jimmy, about to say one thing, at this moment said another. He said to John who sat there agog: "this is your chance." And John raised his right hand in the air and said, "Pardon," but the crew kept going, Moreau kept walking, the reporter kept talking.

Jimmy shrugged then and began his litany of product information once more, but this time John interrupted him, John – spoke – which may have been all Jimmy ever wanted anyway.

"I'm going to be on TV, Jimmy." He said with the utmost certainty and sincerity. "Just you wait and see."

"Why, sure. We're all going to be on someday. That's a law of nature, John. Isn't it?"

"No. No. You misunderstand me, Jimmy. I'm going to be on today."

"How will you do that, John? We'll miss our plane, John."

"Not this one, Jimmy. This one hasn't boarded yet. There's been no announcement to board. And who knows when there's going to be one. No, Jimmy, we won't miss this one. Meantime," he said while rubbing his hands together and becoming less lethargic and more animated as he spoke, "I'm going to chase after that film crew and propose marriage to Jeanne Moreau."

No sooner had he said this, then he pushed the TV aside and was out of his seat chasing after them before Jimmy could utter a word of protest or product information. John caught up to them in a flash. Just like that. He pushed his way between cameraman and sound man. The reporter lunged at him using the large microphone as sword, club, ramrod. John became entrapped in cords, cables, and lights. He fell to the ground while Jeanne Moreau retreated to safety. Then nothing happened. No airport security came to cart him off. Nothing. Nothing happened. She continued her walk and they formed a circle once more about her and proceeded in the same direction toward their destination. John looked up, saw them depart, brushed himself off, and then said quite loudly, "Hath no man here a dagger's point for me?" Some people looked at him; others, looked away. He continued to look in the direction that they walked.

Quickly he changed his clothes. He put on a black mask, a black cape, and black tights. Then he sprinted after them. Once again the reporter lunged at him, protected his lady's honor with the microphone turned now into a pointy spiked mace. This time before he fell he was able to stroke gently her hand. This time he spoke her name. But once again it was the wires and lights more than any other weapon that deterred him from his quest. And once again after he fell, they left and continued on their way without any change as if nothing had occurred at all. "Adieu," John said, "adieu."

Next he put on a polymer face mask and gained fifty pounds. He wore a rumpled business suit and learned a foreign accent. He became Kissinger, though fleet of foot he remained. Now as he neared the sacred circle, the circle opened and welcomed him. He held her hand this time. He, sweetly, though with a certain accent, spoke her name and then proposed. She laughed and then everybody laughed – all throughout Orly Sud everybody laughed for the proposal appeared live on every TV set in the airport, on every TV set in France. Jimmy saw this; he saw John in his Kissinger disguise propose to Jeanne Moreau on TV. The reporter asked John/Henry a few questions. He replied wittily, but vacuously. There was no turn to foreign policy. Then Moreau leaned forward and kissed him on the cheek, a sweet peck. They were off again, continuing quickly in the direction of their destination. John stood there, stared after them, a few people smiled at him. He felt satisfied and removed the mask, lost all that uncomfortable weight, went back to his blue jeans and white high top Converse basketball sneakers, went back to Jimmy.

"Did you see me?" John asked. "Did you see me?"

And Jimmy replied, "I saw you, John. I saw you. But how will they know it was you they saw? How will they know it was you, John, you?"

They sat quietly, even morosely for a few minutes. John sunk back into his seat, pulled the set back into place, watched the screen set before him, screwed, soldered, molded tight to its metal or plastic hard as steel arm. He did not move. He did not blink. Jimmy, though, fidgeted a bit and flipped intently, nervously through his source. He became visibly annoyed, angry even. He said that he couldn't find the information that he wanted to find. He couldn't find out which TV set it says is best. He couldn't do it, but he wouldn't give up. "John," he said. He promised.

9   To the Approval of All Gathered

There was a man with a bag over his head who used to collect trees. He was an artist. In his latest work he did a lot of barking. He barked at people at Orly Sud. They did not know what to do, what to make of this man who had chained himself to the top of a railing and who barked and howled with impunity. The airport security officers stood nearby and watched and laughed every so often at people's reactions to this howling, barking man. And so most of the time since security did nothing, since the man carried on so with impunity – that word again – passersby knew not what to do or how to react. Art should challenge after all. Right?

But the situation became ugly when other artists, the Brothers Oleg, commenced with their newest work which required them to mill about in eighteenth-century dress as Jefferson and Lafayette. Unfortunately, Lafayette wandered too close to the dog artist who became so furious that he broke his chain and barked incessantly as he chased Lafayette around the nearest waiting area. Jefferson tried to come to his friend's aid, but the dog artist lifted his leg and, yes, he peed on the great man, the third President of the United States, Thomas Jefferson, who then ran hastily to the nearest rest room. Lafayette meanwhile accused the dog artist of censorship: "a direct attack against freedom of expression" were his exact words. The other artist at this point broke from his dogged impersonation – so to speak – and declared it all "too much, too much." He'd have no more of it, he said. "Let the public decide." And those in the waiting area proclaimed their favor of the costume spectacle that was Jefferson and Lafayette. Just then the original artist of this artists' space reassumed the genius of his art, that is his dog-like behavior, and turned his ire on the audience. Several people were injured by the sharpness of his teeth or the swiftness of his paws.

The three artists have been invited to exhibit their work in New York. At this moment they are waiting, still waiting for take-off, for wings and other parts, for reverie.

The New Passenger

FROM THE BACK OF THE BUS I could see the front. It was full, but not crowded. It would jerk forward and then it would seem to jerk back as it stopped to gather up more. At the next corner, the bus stopped. It sat there still as a stone right through two or three green lights. "Go. Go!," everybody thought, though no one said it.

Out of a back alley a short, slanted man dressed in green khakis and worn, beaten black shoes ran toward the bus. Just as the bus jerked and rattled a crawl forward, it stopped once again. No one yelled in their guts "go, go," because no one likes to see a driver go past someone who's running to catch up. The driver opened the doors and the man skipped a step on his way in rather than break his awkward stride. He smiled, dug deep in his pockets, and pulled out a monthly commuter's pass. He held the card up proudly. It seemed as if I could see his picture on the face of the card. The driver muttered mechanically, "seventy-cents." The man with the brimming smile said, "pass." And the driver replied like the air-filled machine that opened the doors, "seventy-cents." The new passenger did not understand. He just stood there, silent; holding his pass. The driver tried to explain: "That's no good until next month," but the driver did not understand either. The new passenger just smiled and held his pass higher.

Throughout the bus everyone started to shout "Go! Go, damn it," every way they knew how to without actually shouting it. Feet shuffled, throats cleared; one fellow even punched the seat in front of him as hard as he could. No one knew how many green lights we had sat through. I knew then that I should have walked.

A crowd of people swaying and singing approached the bus. They entered in one mass movement knocking the slanted man sideways and then back into a handrail and then back into the bowels of the bus where I sat. The mass that sang and swayed seemed to have awakened the bus. The driver started again, closed the doors, jerked the bus toward the river. The slanted man had taken a seat. He tapped his feet to the rhythm of the song or the engine gears and smiled, unabashed he stuck those yellow teeth out a mile.

The Age of Discovery

ROUND LIKE A CLOCK. Long like an ear. Round like a sun. And the moon? Hidden by the blue mountain. White lines intersect the brown plain. What do you make of that? So, I said the answer will be unlocked only by way of the vision that you walk in. But their eyes clouded over and the rest of us went beyond the blue mountain in search of Columbus. He sailed; we walked. It's all we're left with despite the two other things that can have no value for the new owner. Repeat. Round like a clock. Long like an ear. Our time would soon run out and all we could do is walk ever toward that blue mountain, high above the brown plain. The other side we imagined as flat, but with more spices and jewels than Zanzibar. John had discovered that. We read his reports while caught in the circle of Samsara that only the one word which was all words could unlock and so we walked, hoping to reach the other side of the blue mountain sometime before sunset. The top was more plateau-like than we imagined and John's reports made little reference to this feature. It was at this point that we first became suspicious. We walked on. Yes, we walked on and on, up that slight incline of the long plateau-like summit. Many of us died. Days passed. When we reached the other side, we slid down the waterfall, made the first known contact with the waterfall people, and lived amongst them. Days passed. Many of them died.

Money Behind Claim

IN DECLARING A REVOLUTION the world is a monument to the alienation of the churches. Turned away by civil authorities, they built their hope of salvation on sweet morsels mixed in such sighs that the soul pauses for the word rather than the ritual. In time the gulf between the spiritual side and the collapse of economic sensibility acts as no other threat of the time. The lessons of the past yield to a willing submission ordinary people pushed to its logical extreme. The right, the need, the assumption that bound them to each other, some honored and some obscure, seemed stripped from a treatise in defense of liberties overseas. For a full ten years, everywhere, they sought to persuade the heart that with a crude directness of speech – vituperation, satire, and all the standard tropes – the revolution could be readily dismissed as mere rhetoric.

With every revolution some new emotional tone for more drastic curbs rallied crusading disillusion into a general instrument for regulation. The whole spirit of innovation suggested reaction that shunted the agitation revived in this shift even if no new grass roots concern proved that the whole pessimistic wrath displayed a much more highly charged exclusion. Instead of struggling, departments served to protect that status quo which had seemed to depend on the war effort. The impulse behind the conflict had often seemed comic, although obviously secret societies developed conformity through fear. This pervasive shift came on the wings of a phrase. They needed painful fervor to fulfill a quasi-military invasion that crystallized long before the spirit of supremacy stood. Time and again, a new phrase cut deeper than economic crisis. A sweeping statement vindicated a conquering nationalism. The general crisis forms nationalistic ones. Gradually, a frozen posture – the keystone of the structure – grants leaders the habitual strut and swagger of the day. Rudely shaken, one can never wholly separate, I think, internal conditions fraught with a matchless fury from the wedge stimulated by the idea of individual freedom. The significant measure of change does not answer such questions.

the hammering of events is without effect
Social reform was vulnerable to the kind of flow it received. Balanced by the reduced wants of people, an inevitable rhythm has an immunizing effect. Savings must also be plentiful; the failures, unimportant. One exception and, unhappily, one the least understood, is the exposure of what auditors fail to find. In later years the slump extended a profound weakness subject to no regulation. But now in an orderly manner buyers pool resources, among other things, and a golden age of management and control established the corporate chain. One of the paradoxes is this reluctance to concede that the end has come in accordance with nothing but money.

The persisting weakness nominated top-bottom polarization. This striking increase conformed to the accommodationist model. In one – which is not to say it involves a loss – particularly ominous disaffection the minority party appears much less inclined to think of themselves as a collectivity in relative decline. Coherence is part of the permanent order of things. Nonetheless, the problem of distinction blocks significant new power.

The end promotes the implementation as well as the formulation of policy. The secret of success, the war. How to approach the revolution, through law. It is safer to reject the fear that all the lingering thousands did not eliminate. But what of those activities the giant points to now? If, when there is no crisis, success has eluded the world twice, then we must conclude that power replaced the move to legitimacy. Of means or of ends, forms lacked access. They are ambivalent; that is well and good – a matter of survival. This is already a criminal act. Insurance companies are far more socially significant. This route led to other factors of production, the fullest vision. Grapple with the apparent. It went into decline.

What you see depends on what you look at and how you look at what you see depends on what you know.

Andre is Dead

WHICH FAMILY MEMBERS watched what? We must begin to discuss what visitors see. Desire is learned. The origin of TV is tied to the development of the telephone. Fairground curiosity, however, became corporate asset. Imperialism, authority, hegemony: which of the three do you find most satisfying? Radio, unlike film, was from the start tied to the military and became inextricably linked to planned corporate culture, the abstract is always rooted in the concrete. A world wide network was only one of the benefits of war. Eddie Cantor got one hundred thousand dollars per minute.

What will Eve say when Adam tells the District Attorney what he saw that night at the swim club? Wealth protects its self-interest and this is good. We identify with them and root for their success. His films, often in color, are the most filmic. Color has little to do with the smoke and fog of working class conditions. Did Phyllis Wheatley write from her own heart or did she write in a manner that matched society's expectations?

When the Grecian states knew no other tools than the axe and the saw, the Grecians were a great, free, and happy people. They made wood resemble stone or flowers and made stone look like trees or vines. Here is the finest ride in America. This of course supports the importance of familial relations. Was Yale the center for education? This leads to a discussion of character; the differences are much more important.

Clara is both historian of and suffering participant in her own drama. The protagonist kills his smaller housing with a larger screen. What happens here to where we started? Orient us, and indicate development. Openings attract the attention of readers and establish expectations. Students speak to other students. Feel free to use the following to help you shape your discussion. What makes James Baldwin's "Stranger in the Village" so good? It is especially dangerous to criticize Israel.

Although in reality situations are usually never so simple, Minneapolis and St. Paul report how much they differ. What I had interpreted as a malicious attempt to embarrass high winds with hedges was merely bewilderment. To write clearly, not only the most expressive, but the plainest words should be chosen. During the next two weeks look for something to analyze. "Public" suggests parameters and thereby an enclosure for the movement. Energy ripples in reverse to settle in a confined center. Neither is this poetry limited to constraints of time. Apparently, the traditional disciplines of literature and history are no longer entirely able to answer certain questions.

Biography

WHAT A NECK-ACHE. You wake up and there it is. You wonder about the Egyptians and Mesopotamians for a few moments. What breakfast did their hands make? What color was her hair last night in the dream that began and never finished? There was that motorized duck decoy that pulled you through the water effortlessly until you let go and boarded the massive ship. You wake up too early because you went to sleep too early and slept restlessly thinking of this page. You were asked again by one to be another. You write the letter; he signs the page. How to imitate? There is no time to follow Bishop Burnet, no time to change appearance with theatrical device, no time to learn a new voice. It is time for the delivery. Its words caught by the moisture in the concrete outside, uncomfortable to the touch, too large for the kitchen table.

You drove the whole way (all nine hours) and you were so tired that it was difficult to order breakfast. You went inside the large dining hall. You were too tired. You just wanted to sit down. No one seemed very certain whether or not they brought the order out to you or if you had to go back to the counter area. You started to read, you started to work on something while you waited. Then the phone rang. It was your father, but you pretended you didn't hear the message and left the phone off the hook and on the table. You wanted to finish what you had started. Then you would speak. It wouldn't be too long; besides someone else could speak for a few minutes – the messenger, the messenger knew you were busy, anyone could see that, the messenger didn't have to walk away and leave the phone. The dining room was full of people.

From the four corners of the globe to the four corners of the room: boxed in. Here is the proof that something survives, that something can be found even in the irrecoverable. This is what lines all those shelves. Return to your game and then the pizza. Three phone calls then and each one longer than the one before; the final one lasts until the early morning. The message of each is unclear. You can only wonder. Early on you wonder what the others think of the tall one, of the quiet one, of the smiling one, of the smart one, of the talkative one, of the fat one, of everyone. And before that the empty box - no word from the outside - the blinking light - one valued message that you trusted because of the sincerity of the voice. Back on the ground again all you can do is pace the four corners of the room, the four corners of the globe, and keep count.

One card here; one card there. A crow's caw wakes you. You are asked how it went. Such questions, you find, difficult to answer. You desire more specificity. The crow has only one thing to say – constant – the stupid, annoying bird. All I can do is wait, you say. Even then, all you can do is wait. In the delays are new opportunities to write. In the delays are chances to quicken the pace.

You speak of the effacement of ego, then write page after page. Every word used and then used up. Some words repeated in each context in such a way that each context becomes the text. Still the void is there. Still the unnameable. Down the stairs, out the door, the whole world is wet. So much to put away. It is a father that all have gathered around. You wash your face – vague recollection. Everything is all set. It has to succeed this time. The other says thank you and nice to meet you. That's all. This is the century's night.

Call then and make an appointment for 4:30 today. Tomorrow two appointments. They seem to increase. The next day none. A pattern of lines and cross-lines, large dark spots as if far off planets' surfaces. Yellow asterisk atop the surface, the slow beat that's almost inaudible, almost out. A deep, but narrow yard with pavement on three-quarters of its side. Next door a room that has chipping paint, broken screens outside and boxes piled helter-skelter ceiling high inside. The boxes belong to someone. Picture them at the beach with their boxes, hiking in the western hills with their boxes, shopping at the mall with their boxes, arriving at the airport with their boxes, alone with their boxes. The shade is crooked; the coat, hung. The construction repeats itself. The front page photograph makes expectation irrelevant. No more trees with bent branches by the window framed. No more red brick. A haircut, a meeting, a short trip in a car. You can hear three distinct whistles, but not name a single one. Here is the robin's call and over there the whippoorwill's. Not true, not all of it – just a percentage. Clapboard and green grass. The crow's – that you know. *To know* ... Is it beautiful to feel? A little more enthusiasm, please, you think, not from you, from all the others who you know are deficient in this regard.

The person on your left answers all the questions. A real go-getter. Others proclaim what's needed and that is always just-what-they-want. Their own petty self-interests. You had forgotten how tortuous and dull these meetings could be. You feel as if you'll jump out of your skin. At the same time, sleepy. Not a pleasant feeling. Why are you here? Wake up. The alarm has sounded. Day has begun. Get outside. The clutches of the panther are better than these proclamations and the go-getter's pathetic enthusiasm. Join a submarine crew. Run silent, run deep. What a pleasure, the quiet down there beneath the waves, every person doing their part to make the thing go. Meanwhile, the collapse, all the issues unresolved. It's your fault, you sleeper, you.

Try to decipher the name at the bottom of the card so that you can reply. Throw the rest out. Pick-up the book and wait for the delivery of three sheets of paper. Play the game for one hour. Fix the hole in the ceiling. Tighten the screws in the door. Look up the spelling of the names, the time of death, and the exact phrase. Drive the car, pack the bags, cash the check. Wait downstairs. Listen to the piano music – twice. Make the phone call. Leave a message. Answer the phone. Listen to a message. Outside everything wilts. Even the sidewalks begin to sag. Downtown has been turned into a ghost town. It's just too hot. The moles dig deeper down trying to find some frozen ground. The mailman sits on a stoop in the shade reading the paper. It's just too hot. It's not the heat but the humidity you say wet from your third shower. Off you go to spackle more holes, tighten more screws, and wait for more calls.

Just a stones throw away is the escarpment that rises like a lone skyscraper over the surrounding land. Rain falls constantly in the east, a torrential rain that darkens the skies for days at a time. Plans must change at such times. Everywhere the signs are posted – "Postponed - Date To Be Announced." At such times people enjoy some specially prepared foods with friends who travel cautiously to meet. It gets so dark that you burn candles as well as turn on every electric light. Sometimes the old songs start spontaneously or the stories of "in the beginning" begin and never end. You might simply read the paper, relax, forget about problems of drainage. There's little you can do. Always by surprise. All that equipment out and ready to go and then the sky opens up. Start when it all stops in a week, two weeks. Then the fog across the fields is so thick that it too stops play. "Postponed" – again. You try to sleep a little longer, but wake up the same time as always. Always at the same time; always at the same place.

Once in a blue moon you'll remember what your not supposed to forget. Get in the proper frame despite friends lost to budgets. One man will welcome you to the lane while another follows you about the house. What's underneath the rugs and is it too far in winter you wonder? Then, all of a sudden, nineteen pages turns into twenty. Everything is a mess except the window that overlooks the backyard. Imagine all the things to put away; the loss of time. You're not in the proper frame. Jefferson at first wrote "the pursuit of property" and only later did he change it to "the pursuit of happiness." He was a wise man and other wise men say one's first guess is usually correct. This isn't what you meant to remember. That was something wilder, brighter, freer. Was it the eagle's soar or the whale's watery plume? Who knows. It's hard enough to remember an address and how to get there from here.

It's another walk up the hill in the hot sun or the storms that pass through late in the afternoon. One day near the top of the hill you found the tattered remains of a weather balloon. Even in war it is necessary to forecast the weather. There are certain activities better suited for rainy days; others, for sunny days. We are together in these enterprises of prediction. You guess that tomorrow will be the day of days.

It's not so much that it's a competitive world, but that people decide to enter the wrong competitions. He didn't like his auction price and therefore sprayed perfume in one of the guard's eyes on his way out. He had too much to drink again. A little disheveled, even his cute smile, family connection, and prominent position could not bring in the very top price. He was one of the very last to go and the only one to get angry, to think of it as a competition and a defeat. This made you toss and turn for awhile. Charity, after all, begins at home. By the roadside flowed an unnamed stream, almost overflowing its banks. There is a hospital in this town so there must be lots of money. The choices are endless. Four galleries; one painting in each gallery. On the top floor, a Magritte depicting the other three floors. There you are entering again. There is a woman up the block in an antique shop who can't get out. She watches you but says nothing. As you walk by you can smell her perfume.

The principles of design are basic: everything turns brown. Just then the hawk returns to bother the crows who only want the tree. Distance increases, top to bottom lengthens as the days shorten. The tall flowers remain favorites. Even here then, where are you? This requires further study and study requires time. Three projects are all that anyone can handle. Consider the other side. The action to be taken is obvious. Plant the tall flowers here where you live; learn their names.

On the inside it was fine, but if you touch it then you'll rip it. Body spackle will repair it, a necessary blood-letting to relieve the pressure. Notice the blue color under the skin. The third or fourth incision will be painful; the ones before and after will not be so. It's always the same. When you shake hands the blood of the other remains. What a mess. No more sailing for at least a week. Grounded. Despite abuse and neglect, a blue heron, a red-tail, an osprey, red bliss potatoes. Bags of different sizes greet you – you're home. Cut the pie in half. Let the cold water run. Pull the car down. See the house painted blue. One small surgical poke won't do. The incisions are a must. It's actually blue, you know, but when it hits oxygen it instantly turns red. That ought to relieve the pressure. Change positions. There's an opening. The sound of bubbles. Don't look now. Try some tin and straw. Can you paddle? Time to make a swift get away.

A train coming down the tracks, a plane about to crash. Danger. Trees falling, the lamp on the pole slanted and about to fall. Danger. Hard to imagine. Right here and now. There it is. Everywhere. A pool filter exploded, destroying the adjacent house. Due to dry weather and winds the flames leapt from this property to those on either side. Soon the whole area of expensive homes burned. Some fled on bicycles carrying what valuable possessions they could fit into a knapsack and saddle bags. An engine on its way struck a telephone pole as it swerved to avoid a collie crossing the road. Phone service was out for more than seven hours. You heard one person say, "When it rains it pours." That, too, irritated you. Everything was slow to respond except flame to flame. The whole world seemed orange and red. Due to dry weather, water pressure was dangerously low. The Captain answered questions. He did not think quick, but carefully. You said let's go. The only word to use is stupid.

The main heartstring ripped. Just some small threads held the pump in place. Meanwhile the assailant had the use of his hands and feet – free to attack again. Parallel lines; perpendicular lines. Slats versus gaps. "In our time the world is pregnant with contradiction," you said and left it at that. Sometimes at night you can hear the lonely and hurt cry out. The wick reaches the bottom, a small wind blows all that's left of the scent out the seven windows. So it is with the spirit. Then there's that mole outside, above ground this time, trying to get inside and take over: the mole from another planet. How do you know? It fits the profile of alien moles. In the library you check facts. There isn't enough water. The final message is on the outside of the envelope. Severed and resown, tell everyone. Once you get going, go quickly. You're on your bike, keeping a safe distance between you and the fox.

Sitting on a bench with a mirror in one hand and a cage in the other, you try your best to trap a bird. In theory it is so simple; in practice, so hard. The idea is that you'll see a bird approaching in the mirror, hold the cage in the proper position, and trap the bird as it flies over your shoulder. Who will close the trap door? In Belgium one sees many scenes similar to this; each one is a lonely pursuit, one never pursued by the stars of the Memphis blues festival, 1969–1970. Undreamt by the hoards at the gate; yet such a simple thing. If a box is empty, why not fill it? If a bird flies, why not trap it? Patience, patience. If not today, tomorrow. Watch the mirror closely. Do not let your attention waver one iota. You are alone on the bench and always will be. Impossible to see beyond the bench and the mirror. Impossible to hear the beating of the bird's wings. Impossible to smell its droppings. Steady the cage now. Something approaches. The sun in the mirror starts a fire.

The sky darkens. From now on the exotic will have to be manufactured; thought, smothered in its infancy. Saw tooth. The sense of being trapped. Turn right, a wall. Turn left, another wall. Turn around and there's nothing there, but who can ever think of turning around. A change of colors must mean something. Smaller print, a disfigured nose. You think he is the ugliest human being on earth. Usually you don't react this way. Now you jump out of your skin, from one void to another. The Gulf of Despair is on every map. There must have been something good. Memory knows only what it recalls. You went ahead and typed more pages until a hawk swooped down and pinned a squirrel. That's a real attention getter. A thousand stops before the castle. Too much time in the car even though less than on other days. Still, no castle. Just the moat and the dragon and the archers, bows drawn, every arrow pointed at you, at your heart, at your eyes.

Take a lake side dock punch after global ice skids on roof parts. You with the vertical hat on a pointy head, you with the red tie. That's the engine in the rock. Broken hearts mend the saw given on two day offers. It's as if the wing wedged itself in the tallest building's highest corner. Drop down. Take a sharp look at Fort Such and Such for the hazards that inevitably await. Won't do much good but it'll give you something to write home about. Deep sleep. You, fellow with the red tie and forgotten suspenders. Take a long walk off a short pier. You and what army? Light half way the dark inside, the hollow of your gut. The stick is sticking up. It's a hold up. Get down below the line. Advance and collect $200. You're out of time, dropped for a loss, blocked. Here at the foul line, fouled. That's no fair. Let's make a deal. Hold on. Water, water everywhere. What did you think. That's the planet. That's your own body. Mostly water.

The wheels on the bicycle started to turn backwards even as it continued to move forward. There was no point in peddling now. In the pool the water had turned a greenish color from the heat. Bugs prospered in the office that had once been yours. The passage of time can be brutal. You turned the outside light on just in case day became night quicker than expected. This you call memories, a perfect idea played up one key. Do you hear the bugs? Stephen is the first to respond. He must be excited about adding this example to his collection: printed, matted, and framed. Sold. Some things move slowly. For example: caterpillars, turtles, the moon up above, yesterday. Follow the ball's bounce to the end of the line or through the hoop. Look, there's more than one-hundred and fifty others kicking it. Ring your bell. Through the glass some will lift their legs; others, their torsos. The magician doesn't show up because he's out of tricks, because his sentences are too short and his phrases too long.

Someone else should do the cleaning, anyone else. You are better at eating. Let's eat. Then there's the photographs and the stories of how you took them. So much to say, so much to explain. What state, what time, what exposure. In the distance there is the woman in white whose attention you try to get to let her know about the house. Someone – whose name you can't remember – boards twenty-eight horses. Does he have to help her with all that? They will return to London together this time. Back in the automobile there is a very strong smell of onion or garlic. It reminds you of something else, but you can't remember what – or whose? The thought of it for six hours makes you feel sick. Back out in the air two children run by in pirate costumes. They pretend they don't know you. They pretend they're pirates. Instead of swords, though, they brandish popsicles – one cherry and one blue. The floor is brown linoleum, the color of the trail taken to get to this point, this place in time. The blue-green water perfectly matches that which rolled into the shore during your walk, perfectly matches the color of the one-eyed snake carved into her arm.

The unhinged shopping cart gathers up every loaf in the store. It runs wild with lentils. A sudden explosion by the door stops it. A fruit smell remains after its misadventure. Pepper blackens the walk where it became so unsettled that all its contents dispersed in several different directions. Meanwhile, there are other fragrances to contend with such as that of damp newspapers. Short sentences also have their own peculiar odor. See if you can lengthen or alter yours as a way to send them off the track, a way to keep them off the property and to provide you with some more space in which to move. After all, everyone asks for too much money. Trying to remember, you feel, should be a paid activity, not a voluntary one. It takes time to recall messages and time is money. Everyone has their own system of saving. Cocktails became popular during World War I. Wine grew in popularity after World War II. Tea and coffee, on the other hand, have long been popular.

Everything is out all over and guess who pulls up? Here for some "refueling." You run upstairs and put on the jeans that were on the floor. No time for underwear or shoes. They're making noises outside already, talking loudly about how the left hand page is always shorter than the right hand page, arguing about the reason for this. You have had dinner already; the dishes are all over the place. Tonight you ate with no clothes on. There is no time to clean up anything. Barely time to run upstairs, throw on the jeans. Make some coffee. Let them eat the leftovers, fight over them by denial. No one mentions the current situation – a near crisis or so it looks – they just continue chewing. You close a window. Something to do – meanwhile. It all feels like a missed opportunity to you. Their plates are so clean you won't need to wash them. All gone. No more. Would anyone like more coffee?

Something about retaking a castle from a larger neighbor. You will sleep on it. Try to remember it. A different place. The smallest country. Something about just enough soldiers to make sure the others can get back. No one will stop them. This is purely ceremonial. The rest you cannot remember. The old Roman walls. What's left of them. One wide avenue. A deep, deep sleep. All of this written on demand. There are reasons why each should have his own. There are things stuck to the sink. You see the hill and the sun rise over the hill. This used to be. You get up to all the sounds outside. There was never a town beach across the street so the restaurant must have moved during the past few years. A slip of paper falls to the ground. As it falls, you catch just a few words: "begin a new career." A soldier perhaps or a Roman? Maybe a ceremonial wall? Instructions on how to return: follow the winding path, place all references at the end of each essay, go back to sleep. What is this desire to be somewhere other than where you are now, here? In the background, inmates hooted at the marks at the top of the page, at the noise coming up from downstairs, at the cheater. Unplugged, spilled, dropped: one thing after another. To be on an island. To increase the number. There happens to be nowhere to go in this flood. Open the gates. Look inside. Now concentrate on the stretch of a single thin line across the drenched horizon, but that line does not exist and the storm continues its fury, its fervor. Right before you left, set sail, you made this recording. Some will laugh, some will be frightened, some will listen. "Has the right cup been used?" From Michigan a message left on the machine asking you for suggestions. After a walk, the pad fills with answers. After a walk, little uncertainty. Then the mind suddenly becomes a box and when you look inside the mind suddenly empties itself of all it held and the inmates cheer, yelling "cheater! cheater!"

Nobody ate their box lunch because they complained of bad headaches. You wondered what would happen to the food. Keep it short to make it memorable. Legs like a thoroughbred. Then the collapse. You sleep badly knowing what the future occurrence will be. The students' eyes cannot be met. If only their parents knew, but what difference would the knowledge make, you wonder? The aquatics instruction might be of some value to a few and only a few gather about the instructor, too few. You say nothing. What could you say? The cookies remain out there on the table undisturbed. Those headaches. One second the wind blows, the temperature drops, and it rains. A moment later there's a fireball sun in the sky and no one moves outside for fear of frying their skins. This is one of the busiest times for the library. The eggs delivered to local stores still look edible though you doubt that even this appearance will continue much longer. It starts first with the horses, then occurs with the dogs, and finally it reaches you. The thoroughbred has been shot, its headaches had become unbearable.

What is it like to be you? Less negative about the whole planet? You saw him locking up his office last night and didn't know what to make of the fact that he had found a new car on his own. It was so dishonest, so impetuous. You paced back and forth in the hall all during the intermission. You have your heart set on obscurity. The newsworthy will be abandoned. There will be other opportunities to put one word after another. Already the large chain stores have had trouble with the twentieth letter. What you don't know won't hurt you. At the top of the stairs the conductor waited, swinging his arms this way and that. Two guitars now, both silent. A home in Pennsylvania. You brought the basketball into bed early, very early in the morning. Your feet were sore and you had forgotten the words of a favorite song. A note tacked on the refrigerator door would serve the function of memory for a short time. One person leaves; another returns – everything slightly off to the side so that none of the keys can open any door.

Out of the mouth of the cave, a new monster. A rust color now. Later, near completion, a dull gray. Up the hill the bricks are red, the grass is green, the trim is white, all is neat and clean, a picture perfect Edenic little world away from the rust and the boards that have replaced all the glass windows on the other side of the river. Out toward the sea the vacationers plot their moves on the game board blue of calm water. You see a train go speeding by and then an hour later, a second train. Each time a small boat moves toward the trestle, circles, goes back where it came from, goes out of your field of vision. It does not go under the trestle. And there are few objects of any kind near the mouth of the cave. People look quickly toward it, see the flame, and avert their eyes. In the small village it seems nothing has changed in eighty years. All energies of change have been sacrificed to power the torch of the cave. You hear talk of improved rail systems, but are skeptical. You walk among the stones searching for signs of the standard creatures that patently go with such a scene.

From the center of the circle such plump fruit. It costs so much money to get in here and even more to get out. An artist of temperatures and sluggishness with a bad taste in the mouth. What remains after the black and red bowls, the pink cards and full-throated sounds of desire? Another day through the park, past the chimneys uncounted, back from plains of pavement to the objects to be put away. Yellow broth in the red and black bowl. The phone rings or it doesn't. You answer it or you don't. Forty-four years in one house is too long a time. It is only the car that you like. Otherwise, there are too many stripes. During the flood few will walk, but how else will you get from here to there? It costs so much money to get out of the flood. The body shakes at the thought of the expenditures. You fill up your cup at the trough and await the motor car. Questions to be answered with closed eyes. A number for every question; a ring for every answer late in the night, early in the morning, very early in the morning.

Make a note of the philosophical texts that scratch at the back of your throat. Remember what you did with the memory of sundry items listed, noted. The exact hour of departure; the precise moment of return. The promise to visit again. The tapes replayed, studied. The hours at the desk broken by a walk in the rain. One especially long paper required an extra large staple. The laws of nature. Try to breathe more through the nose when writing. It may have been popcorn and not philosophy that stuck at the back of your throat. You sneezed then, thankfully. Systematize the mornings: start east and head west. Are there any mornings that you have forgotten? Is it possible to ask? Here's a new address. You plan to drive by later that night but hours later you realize you don't have a car.

One light over the left shoulder and one light over the right: balance, symmetry, calm in the day even if the day is dark as night.

The throbbing in the veins matches the sound of this new place. The laws fill the margins. The board by the beach tells you so. This is cheating, but think ahead, land on your feet, plan for the future and try out the future plan. There are so many variables, so much to take out of all those parenthetical statements. Today it has not been necessary to cite other remarks. The clock between your eyes says nine o'clock. Let him know. There are many variants. Whose lips will whisper the essential fact? Not yours. No one will take the year and move it to the end of the line where you think it should be.

Then there's the yellow light through the bars and grates. The jigsaw pattern begins to disassemble. One project must be begun before another ends. Get a new bag to put it in in the future. Carry the bag with you. You need a break from fish. Will you have to give this up too? You never saw anything like this. Then there are the people who have returned from trips. They block your path. You want so much to finish early and to do that you must have a clear path, must put everything in the right box or file. Everything smells of fish. It is summer. The potato salad has on occasion been the best part of it. So it too will be over, nailed shut from the outside? Take it as it comes. Today you can tell the story, fill it up with objects of detail so treasured by some. "Action is character." You pin something to the wall, but the wall becomes a train that leaves you standing there in the station.

"Try this" – you believe to be two stupid words but you can't communicate this adequately enough to annoy and because you can't (or don't) everyone thinks that you are so nice. The water drips in the sink; everything smells like leeks. There's no connection. Don't be stupid. The bad smell in the car cannot be precisely named. Dogs bark in the distance and from their bark alone they cannot be named. The lipstick is too red. It must mean trouble. Who has an airplane out at this hour? It is three AM. You have changed your format. Something predicts it. You had to eat quickly.

You had to spell it out once and for all. You had to pick it up. On the run again. He's outside before you're ready. You take everything home. You take everything period. Up close the paintings look gaudy, amateurish. Bus loads of people arrive, every room is booked. New Mexico, New Jersey, New Orleans: it makes no difference at all. You are only so many inches tall and from the number alone no one can say your name. No one can repeat your number.

You've said nothing about the park: the roses, the tall flowers, the circles that you walk. The voice becomes mechanical, inhuman or dull. Do people actually talk about the sermons? All keyed-up to old words? Silence? Crooked attachments to walls? Everyone has two clean starts in their lives – on average. Not enough here beside boredom, they say. The cortege is the last one. Make it off angle in the frame for a little more interest when you come in from work. Evoke glory with the piano. Evoke glory, glory before it's too late, before the guest arrives. Discover the daughter's name. Too much discussion already: try this or look at that. Go to the building, the back, the car salesman. Someone, somewhere needs supplies. Join the ranks. The finger points at you as you walk by the sign and there are so many of them this year. Property matters. Property is matter itself. By the door everyone shakes hands and smiles; some hug embarrassedly. No one says anything about what he said, about what she said, about what you said. Certain words remain unspeakable. These are the most important. These are the undiscoverable laws.

All the heavy, singing people attended. Some swayed. You made plans for ensuing occupations. Prices had not changed. This place and its garden: the heart of paradise. One moment here – invaluable! You wrote to the hermit of the city. The round object; then two round objects: the papers, the basket, the copies, the return. Followed by new ideas and incomplete information left there overnight on the sofa. What remains used, made into a fine thing. Sitting, then standing. The recycled paper becomes cardboard or something made of wood. The short ride, the look inside. No cancellation. How do the children do it? Such patience and then up so early the next day. How did it finish? One thing is certain: one thing remains. The announced sign did not exist. The prize could not be won; even so, no one drove off glum. One complained constantly about accounts and silences, yet even he planned to read all about it and to return. Start your engines. The repaving soon begins.

You better go now while you can. It'll be hours before the hills in the distance start their rise again. You will go down. Perhaps too fast. You'll want to slow down, your brakes insufficient. Then the road will flatten for a moment before it points you and shoots you arrowhead down, flying. Still, all the time, on the infrequent flats or while going down, in the distance, way off, you can see those hills rise up mighty and verdant and you wonder how in the world you're supposed to get up those. That is all you remember. It seems like just moments later, but you are up and over, safe on the other side. The last leg of the travel cannot be recalled at all. Here you sit now at the table planning another journey, one of even more particularity, density, one of no flats whatsoever. The package has been delivered and received. Everything has gotten through, everything checked off on that list and that list now destroyed. Another list begins. Someone, somewhere counts on you. You must go down to the bottom of the hill, the very bottom of the hill, before you can come back up.

Then you put your shorts on. Lots of clothes. You drive, but hardly look at all: they and theirs. One book of travels, one book of philosophy, and one short one of what you loosely call *prose*. Then the farmer starts to harvest his fields. You slept an hour late and missed all the most memorable moments. He left, boarded ship in a bright new uniform. Out on the sea they met up with many similar ships. You did not mention certain things in the newspaper. The conversations were short this time, but certainly not curt. Then you tore some lettuce and put it in a bowl for the salad. You put three carrots on a paper towel. You never did use those carrots. There's a picture of a woman with a pan of some kind in her hand and she stands near what is clearly a stove of some sort. The house is rubble. One of the first to have been destroyed. Lights out. The anticipated storm arrives several hours late. Whatever happened to the fright that accompanied the possibility?

The car stalls and you get out to look for the missing part. Someone has put clean, rolled socks in the fuel line, covered the rear window in masking tape. This could slow you down, but you have to be out of here by nine o'clock, you have to be long gone before the funeral begins. They're coming now in their gray coats and black gloves. They'll exchange rings. In your closet all your shoes have been tied together. They've thought of everything to slow you down, to make you late, to keep you here. Everything has been unplugged, there isn't any milk in the refrigerator, the newspaper is at the top of the hill, the pen is out of ink, the toilet won't flush, there isn't any hot water. They've thought of everything – even your toothbrush seems to be missing. They want you to wear a hat and gloves, they want you to look your best. You refuse. Silently, you protest. There isn't much you can do. They want you to ride in one of their cars. They walk around so slow, so slow. They want you to be the life of their party. They need to have some fun.

Another car at another intersection; another turning point that becomes a vanishing point. You run up hill into the sun – it seems – into the sky. This doesn't last forever. No day does. No hill does. No sky does. Nothing does. Nothing lasts forever, you remind yourself as the binding breaks, as the yellowed paper crumbles in the *Complete Works*. You decide to sell everything before it rots, to take what you can get for it and cut your inevitable losses, but you look inside one book and find there a treasured signature. Back on the shelf it goes: and then another and so on. Time does not stop for you; it keeps running out on you. A stop sign faces you as you reach for your slippers. This is significant. This is the end, you think. Get up, wash your hands, start over again. There's someone at the door or soon there will be. Do not say hello. Just imagine her there and cut your losses while there's still time. Go upstairs, turn into the last room, throw out the book that you have signed.

There's a shadow across the page. Things keep happening to you, though none of them are very important. There are flowers to prepare for the flower show and then there's the surprise book, a study of the word "book," a word that you find so odd. You go out on a new road just to connect with the same old one anyway. After a brief conversation by the flag pole you go to the door, but no one answers. By this time your long book grows shorter; you do not become impatient when you copy over a page for the third time, when you add one missing fact to another. Then the page becomes darkened once again. It is a mystery, it is a portent. You can't figure it out: no power surge or bulb shaking in the lamp, no cloud in the sky or wind shaking trees by the window. An odd dinner causes unpleasant reactions that evening. The command cannot be remembered. Troops plan; troops land. Some still prefer the bayonet, some still carry a cheap mess kit, some still look for a place to camp each night.

Give up then the jovial hand to take the long shot chromatic. Plunge anticipation into the moment unsung for heroes of praise and distinction. This is today and the memory of the before time remains a proof to be read in subsequent times. A letter has been sent; an answer, anticipated. Lost in the lights the return comes right where you stand, lucky you. Can it be completed? The requirements are one screen, a pair of sneakers – not too tight, an envelope substantially larger than its contents, a telephone in good working order, one paperback novel, and a slice of raw sea bass. That should do it. Ride now over the hill quickly before the sun rises, before the soldiers rise. So many sirens, so many likenesses. Everything begins to sound foreign or incomplete, but you let slip the one word that couldn't be said in such circumstances as these.

It must have been a daydream then and yet the comments that Freud made are also incomplete. It becomes a competition, a goal marked out, charted. From here to there requires so much commitment, so much fuel.

Standardize everything: the black wing of the black bird, the perimeter lines of the court, the miles per gallon, the words per page. It is a convenience and a guarantee. Already the plan backfires due to a lack of guarantees, an unclear map, inclement weather. You say that you want to improve your play, but then why don't you follow the guidelines set out in the text? In order to be different you ask for error free copy and a six pack. The route by the old house has been closed for road work. A favorite short cut provided valuable extra minutes that allowed you to move several strikes closer to completion of the daily quota. You changed from pants to shorts for just this purpose. Then the machine so overpowered you that you became dizzy and that dizziness effected the entire afternoon. Conversations, cordial but hurried. Everyone, it seems, is from the same country, everyone tries their best to stretch things. Back on the shelf goes the book; back in the tree goes the bird. Everything is neat. Everything is guaranteed.

So many missed connections through the three gates: two opened and one locked. Calm water and the water story completed on sore legs, stiff joints stiff from smashing down on the blue floor. The paper completed and filed and the circle cut open. The mind enlarged and improved through the ingestion of the necessary liquids. Then all is so quiet. The old route chosen for its familiarity, but surprisingly a heron lands, looks about, and takes off again heading northeast. Someone else sleeps in the field. He's got just a pair of shorts on and doesn't seem to notice the heron. The music of flight is so pretty. Several people discuss their approach to writing. They mention advantages and merit, but never fault, error, weakness. What doesn't work? Up the hill a new guest arrives, but he stays only briefly, only long enough to telephone his next stop and let them know that he is on his way. In the office building everything is quiet today. Not a single light flashes. The bat and ball are where they should be, everything is where it should be.

Everything forgotten; not just the crowded breakfast, but the trips back and forth; not just plane flights and the play with the ball, but the tool box and the stairway, too; not just the new passenger, but the price of a ticket. One trip below for purchases goes as smoothly as can be expected by anyone. On the court everything is quiet, a mild breeze and too many mosquitoes. Packing and unpacking bags over and over again you reach into one and pull out an ancient totem. There is an appearance of cleanliness, but this is not to be trusted. After preparations a suggested idea, a suggested plan becomes the very thing to oppose: a crowd, a lot of noise and commotion. Someone anonymous clears this mess. Out in the night there may have been stars, but no one looked up to see – another busy time of packing up and goodbyes. Engines start, the dark colored cars packed with somber faces move along down the bumpy road. When they stop their contents will be spit out, will disperse in different directions like a sad comet dying.

So sad – the silence between movements. It begins again. The music fills up the room. You will lose your breath. You felt that she didn't care anymore and now you don't care; so at rest, so happy just listening to the music. Then you grab your nephew and hold him as another swell comes pushing the ship up, pulling the ship down, covering the deck in cold, slippery water. Your stomach hurts from the sudden violent motion and all of this happens by the wharf, the old wharf near the caves. Along the shore in the distance from the mouth of one of the caves one of the bearded cave dwellers waves goodbye. The ship has broken free from its moorings and drifts seaward. The towers of the city begin to recede. It is a violin concerto that concludes and having concluded you turn and switch off the old brown radio. A sudden stillness then; the ocean becalmed, the sky dark but without a single star. The smell of the hall of monkeys, its tropical warmth and sour taste, gone. The air cooler than expected. The other passengers asleep, quiet like the pages of a book waiting to be opened, waiting to be read by you slow, wandering reader.

The line between intention and accident blurs to no reclaimable demarcation. Yet, that yodel sound is what it is; no more sense to it than a yo-yo. Foreign phrases such as "beau geste" and "beau monde" appear across the top of your desk. You don't know what to make of them, do you? Great pioneers can hardly be surpassed; so you decide to silence them, to pretend that they were not eloquent. If they try to speak again you will beat the table with both fists, you will scream one continuous indecipherable note. You ask the route to freedom? Skip the interview; try any vein in your body, try any coupon for saving your own pale skin.

The bottom line is always difficult to read. The letter received at night mentions a prior one but that he sent to a different address. The same page appears again and again – an unwanted space, a need italicized, a "t" floating mid-line. It is a nightmare, a disaster. Everything else meets the schedule. Others can worry about permissions now. The night air is delicious. The language you study is foreign. The distance is not quite as long as you thought it would be. How many different songs have used the phrase "once upon a time"? Every record has been played; every book on the shelf, read. At the end of the net some place a device to start the process over again. They are fans of repetition. They do not see it as a trap, a box, a frame. Here in the morning, very early in the morning the number of messages can be refined, the unwanted boxes can be eliminated. Variation will be encouraged. Switch hands, run off in the other direction, do not complete this sentence. Each line brings back a memory, each itinerary brings back an entire era. The order never was haphazard.

The words have a certain magnetic power. What leaves the shelf returns to it – pulled, drawn, forced back into it. Something about communication and its absence occurs to you as the dust from the bookcase causes you to sneeze one last time before the alarm rings. You are up already, you are so eager to begin that all night long sleep brought visions of boxes waiting to be filled, marching boxes open so wide that they threaten you with their cries of "shipment: this side up." The knick-knacks have eyes that follow you from one room to the next, from one night to the next. What does this have to do with school? Twice a day the soldiers clean their rifles; twice a day the principle asks for a one word answer: "yes." But you write the word on the wrong page and then all the rifles, all the eyes turn toward you. The alarms ring. A fat hand grabs you by the throat and puts what's left of you on the highest shelf.

Hundreds of logs break free, then roll down the hill smashing everything before them. They roll at different speeds on top of one another as they descend. Smoke rises from the side where others were once not too long ago. Smoke rises from the chimney at the bottom of the hill, from a chimney of the small house. Inside you turn, you roll also. You sweat and feel chilled. You can see the logs turning, rolling, fast approaching. You get up to wipe the sweat away. Soon you can hear the thunder of the logs. They never arrive – these logs from nowhere, these agents of destruction. There is no house to protect you and no fire to warm you. There is no hill stripped bare of all growth, stripped bare and smoldering. As far as you can see the ground has flattened now into an endless plain. Everything is horizon. It is impossible to see where the two horizons meet. Someone arrives on horse back. You shake hands and then step inside right before it starts to rain. A fire warms the house and you sit in chairs made of tiny logs.

She stood off to the side but couldn't decide which way to face. You went about your business until something tragic occurred. Then everything stopped. The room had a peculiar odor and a yellowish light. For some reason the one thing you remember more than anything else is a mess of black wires that jutted from one wall. For a short time their eyes stared at you with interest, but then your last word caught them off guard and seemed to have caused them some discomfort. It was just one word that so derailed their complete and enthusiastic appreciation of what you had accomplished that night. When you got up your right foot tentatively touched the ground to make sure it was still there, to make sure they hadn't pulled the ground out from under you. The next door neighbor wanted to play, too. Why not? You have two gloves and can't play catch alone. Then you realized your neighbor had been there in the room, off to the side, in a short white costume. Everything goes around in circles, you thought as she ran from home to first to second ...

The exhibit began the day before the company arrived. It would continue for little more than one month. The red in the composition used for the announcement particularly interested you since bright colors evoke an automatic response somewhere deep in the heart of your body and since that red had to have been the brightest of all the colors used in that somber work. Would you call it a drawing? Your friends also received word of the opening and so there was no need for you to call anyone on the phone about this matter. It is a relief not to have to use the phone, it is a relief to get on the right bus and to get off at the right stop, it is a relief to have arrived before the gallery closed for two days. So many arrangements to make just to catch a bus. Everyone wanted to see his work, all the guests, and all of them saw it.

They played hangman with your name all through dinner. No one could guess the right letters. Poor fellow. Then they brought out the food – all of which you couldn't eat. You hid under the table and they forgot about you while they exchanged their tales of travel. When they got ready to leave you popped up smiling like the master's puppet. No one noticed that you had changed your clothes. At the social club the two tall, heavy set men still tuned their guitars. Two hours of tuning, how long they must play? Everything from the back seat had been thrown into the front. You saw yourself briefly in the rear-view mirror and thought your grin stupid, oafish. By the cabin a fog had descended and inside there was an unmistakable odor of damp wood that made you think of canoeing on Lake Arrowhead. On your desk was a letter that required a response. That would have to wait until you got back from your walk, until the books had been delivered, until the dough had risen and been shaped, until the band packed its instruments, until all the papers had been sorted and boxed.

All broadcasting ended late last night with one last rerun of *The Lucy Show*. Someone nearly sent you flying as you climbed down into a brick courtyard by the pointed grates on the outside of the windows. You assured the person that you meant no harm. Luckily, no one in this building had a rifle or a revolver because since the state of emergency started it has been shoot first everywhere. As you descended the face at the window called down to you, "bite me." You're certain those were the words, but you have no idea why that request. At the bottom you found an old cement stairway that led down to a sub-basement near some old, unused stables. There was no loose debris and so you decided to stay. At first you had started out of the city, but then you thought that even though there would be more chaos in the center of the city there would also be more access to such essentials as medical supplies. So with fifteen minutes left you retraced your steps and found this secure place near the southeast section of docks, but not too close to the water.

That town will never be the same again. From the south the new model luxury cars arrive to park on the green and cart the bandstand off to a well-manicured lawn of even-length grass. The drivers all have perfect hair and perfect eyes. Outside the veterans wear caps to hide the zig-zags drawn deep into their scalps by too many years here without the flow of sufficient capital. All that will change. The entire square has been lined with opportunities awaiting the magic touch of the wealthy and the wise. Up the hill, at the top of the hill there is a church school. Children come out of the school dressed in uniforms, marching in double file. The people in their cars parked on the green stare in disbelief. Then the mayor arrives in a fresh straw hat, smoking a cigar. Children wave hello, but the mayor ignores them. No one on the green leaves their car. They're waiting for night to fall so that they can seize the day. Opportunities like this seldom occur within commuting distance of the city. The mayor hands out buttons that say "Vitality!" You have brought your camera.

There's an empty space now, a cavernous hole where the towers once stood. On one tree all the leaves are gone already and on another, one thin branch projects its yellow leaves downward. So many stories have been boxed while others just stood and watched. Every house tells you who has died, although oddly today in one parents spoke of the birth of their child. Wherever you go they ask you to bring the handmade bread and to move into the house just as it is now. Silence on the fields except for the plane above that circles with a message for the banks. Back inside the ground floor smells reminiscent of tomatoes. The warm water covers you after you put away the unused items. There are more stories told about the boy lost in the city, about the visitors to the last fair, about unchanging weather. Someone comes down the stairs throwing sharp glass objects; under the table you go wishing that you had bought the house with the bombshelter in the basement. You have brought a favorite book with you today as instructed. It is *The River Queen*, illustrated. You begin with the first sentence, but have run out of time.

You were too close to the window. The driver couldn't see. He was frustrated and scraped the bottom of the car on a high curb. There was no indication that it was a one-way street. It was. Lines and marks make the information sent stuffed in a box padded with newspaper. First you numbered pages in pencil and then you ran around in a figure eight. You waited on line and became frustrated that you had to wait. You said, "Excuse me. But …" and no one moved for you. At the house now lightened by the donation of its contents, you completed the final task and then left once more. By the curb a silver car had been stripped of all its parts, except its body. That is where you parked and waited. You stood in the hot sun of the late afternoon and waited. Cars came by, entered, and either parked or drove right back out of the parking lot. A tow truck came for one car. Its owner sat next to you on the green window seat. From inside someone tapped on the window and asked you to leave. You sat and waited. You drew lines on a placemat. You can't get out of it that way.

You interview him at some length on matters related to confidence in the granting of wishes. You are now on good terms with the old man. You ask him if he will tell you the story of his life. You wish now to discover on what combination of maps will the limits of the instrumental act depend. You have demonstrated which sums form that model. You may smile at the simplicity of some of his assumptions. You examine change more closely. You suspect, but cannot prove, that the development of the technique is already yielding results. You are now led directly to the question of relationships. You may start out with zero. You shall take the subject up in more detail. You should be content to say that a thing no longer exists, that a new thing has come into existence. You should not labor a point already made. You have been considering the ways in which measures operate to cause or prevent disorder. You examine the reciprocal effect: the ways in which dollars and cents have innumerable tasks. You speak of the unity of all things. You close the book and gaze at the stars and read there every word you have written in your illustrious career.

You point to the notches cut into the edges of the earth. The word "and" joins you to them, to their deepest hollows, to their widest grooves. Somewhere a bell rings; the source unknown. There is a light on below. The door opens before expected, the door opens to the water on the outside causing the ship to sink. The old book has been thrown out – its pages reduced one by one, so many inches of fat. Even the air you breathe is unnecessary. None of the machines will work and the policy regarding them remains to be clarified. No one will call out the name of the pump. The instructor must cry out "Centrifugal! Centrifugal!" The late roses must grow taller in order to bloom. They are the last roses, they are called "the roses of love," you remember. There is hardly enough loose tea to make one last cup and yet it is too strong. Outside someone's hand brakes squeak as he rides down the hill toward the cliff. There are three large trees in the front and at least two more in the back. They will outlive you. Once your arm grew stronger. Imagine a thin branch: frail, thin, brittle, unshakable.

You dream of figs. You dream of an entry stamp placed on a removable page in your passport. You dream of reasonable train fares and short distances. You dream of Brueghel the Elder's *Census in Bethlehem*, the sunset and the ships. You dream of all the ancient wonders, the majestic altars, the half-day visits to places whose names you'll never remember. You dream of the palace of kings and of all the things you'll never know, not even see: the gardens, the coast, the cathedral towns, the oldest buildings, counties and landscapes and the remnants of a passion crushed. You dream of international calls and the strains of jazz. You dream of holding back the flood of the North Sea; you dream of the dance. You dream of saving money. You dream of what it must have looked like before the war and during the first day of the war; of the peace that followed, of the carnival each April. Here you are: asleep in the square beneath the arms of Atlas, tried by an absent jury, found guilty of loitering, of not contributing, of breathing too much air, of taking up too much space, of always rushing off to the bathroom, of complaining, of not speaking the language.

The green pen, how you loved its ink. Every word must struggle for its place in the world; each phrase must avoid the emptiness of cliché. To talk of green ink becomes one way to do so, one way to establish the monumentality of each page. Then there will come a time when someone mentions number and shocks the listener with such paltry figures. Resignation declares itself the captain of this life. Humility turns out to be another name for the dead end signs at the start of every new street. The tires can't take the spiked road, the wings won't float in this electric air. The green ink clears out the images of animals that once kicked out the trainer's cruel brains. The green ink recalls the flood, the attack, the pestilence, the fire, the horror. And you loved its ink, drank it up instead of this region's cherished wine. Celebrate the memory of the night, call it "liberation day," change sides at your convenience. In the square the singing woman still cradles her pigeons in arms held wide apart. She will stay this way for hours; perhaps, even forever – awash in green ink.

The sky has perforations. The bus stops far outside the perimeter of the village, it won't turn in from the main road. From the stop you must walk up the hill, around the curve, through the rain, to the center, and there – like a blessing – spread out before you will be the sea.

Over and over again the bells rang in distant places evoking strong emotions. What happened to a pronounced mystical and perfectionist outlook? At first the typical experience in accordance with private revelation came vouchsafed to all. Because better experience had coercive means, the rivalries had the inevitable heavy hand laid down. It was clear, this combination within encloistered industriousness had thus stood in the forefront of enterprise. An impetus to ventures of their own went hand in hand with a stern view of any pastime as a snare. Indulge the minority given to speculation, to a life of shipwreck and capture. There is no question that a matter of fact language consciously or unconsciously robbed the mind of an intimate connection with the traffic in scientific ideas. The sexual became their faint but perceptible defense of political life. They came to the realization that compromise had chapters that one can cite. Beneath the stars small leaves floated on top, moved in various directions pushed by the quiet current that the breeze created in its passing. The records mentioned above make a schematic understanding instructive.

She removed the tack from out of your back – only a little blood, nothing worrisome. You decided to save it *just in case*. It must have come – somehow – from the photocopying. You could feel it. She told you that there's a hole in your back. Even looking in a mirror, you couldn't see this hole, but you could sense it. Proprioception. Then there were the sirens again, outside not too far away. The blood stopped. Other problems followed. The grinding machine wouldn't stop. You awoke suddenly. Around the circle everything became very still and quiet. Many plans had been changed so that a *program* could be established. After eating, again, the phone calls; the papers in triplicate, the brief conversation face to face, the search for information, the hot coffee. In the study the poems inspired by the voyage disappeared from the screen with one tap of a finger. Outside later that night the conversation turned to benefits and liabilities. Who can predict the outcome?

This is out of order. Time ran out for all that should have been done. You sat on the bed weeping. After the papers, the wash, the deposits, the goodbyes, the purchases, the travel it became impossible to complete the assignment. The doors had been locked, perhaps for the first time ever. A needed volume had been packed in the third box down in a stack of boxes. One plane never came and another arrived thirty minutes late. Around the circle – once again – everything became quiet as the cars filed through the gates. What to do about schedules? You took the machine out of its steel casing, lifted it back into the casing, and then removed the entire apparatus. Decisions about colors are difficult, but at this point such decisions would be premature, out of order, not yet necessary. There'll be extra chairs in the circle, planned activities, dictionaries of words. Don't get too excited. Sit on the steps and wait as others walk in and out of the red brick building. Sit on the steps and predict how long you have left to live.

It's early to bed, early to rise. It's finding the right way without making a wrong turn. Flipping through the pages, spitting out the words, smashing the eggs, cutting deep into the circle: all these things. Hold your left hand on the page so that the right hand can move across it. Create a new design or copy a successful one. In the margins it gets lost. In the margins remember sitting, napping, typing, the walk in the park with special attention to the roses and the tall flowers, the ride past the house with such mature hedges – "how old they must be" – the turn in the lot and the return to more eating, sitting, talking. And that which did not get said becomes the plan for tomorrow, a sign out at the end of the drive with an arrow pointing. The flowers become more fragrant; the city, revitalized. Then, all of a sudden, there's more light. After all, there's a space between words; a space for light, air, time; a space to grow in and to move around in, to recall. In the margins remember; in the spaces between words project the future. Here's where cosmology comes into play.

When you returned to the car the seat burned your back. The coffee mug had not been well-rinsed and the taste of detergent repulsed you. How can you judge a person just by the tone of her voice on the answering machine? The folded piece of paper became a little football kicked by a finger across the room. Its message had not been read and in the future there would be unknown books and essays also unread, also kicked by fingers across a room. Then out of one of the four cardinal directions came the best answer: this we called "genius." You have one page. What will you do? You must not cross-out, you must not disgrace the fantasy of genius. Once in the lower field by the cross of salvation stood those three annoying letters in sculptural forms of extraordinary size. One will lean against another; one will say to the other that this has all been said before, this has all been said before.

Over the Latin, perhaps. Over the dreamed of new books. Connecticut. After wandering feeble and diffuse. To gain homage not to forego the circumstances. Good is a subject in its most force avoiding deceit, an erroneous or imperfect ancestry. Supplied with an object, at first terrified by the perils exposed, industry had now enabled leisure, a rock whose sides were steep, but allowed that constantly assigned disobedience to be drawn from these facts. Temper was scarcely a topic. Tarnish an obvious resemblance, admire the performance. The testimony of senses haunted solemn fate. Wonder argued a diseased condition of understanding that a ray from above would dispel in attractive colors. The good that would arise might be inferior to your objections. But this was not all. Obedient to impulses, how little at length you whisper. A pit incontestably aggravated the cause of this rhetorician. Sway with energy through the impenetrable secrecy; conjecture. Some fatal conclusions have biassed your estimate of sight. The ambiguity of that concealment ends in a manner suited to virtues. It was of no use.

What does the parrot say in the pet shop? Orange is a good color. This is out of place here. When do you introduce the speaker to the listeners; when does the speaker sing? The purple light spreads out across the sky. What makes a sentence interesting and for whom? You do not know the color of the sky nor the key to the sentence. Nothing will get you there in time. You'll have to stay overnight, you'll have to save money. A walk ends in an easy chair long before its planned termination. More conversations. Some donuts then whose coating sticks to the fingers. Some debate regarding originals follows and you return again to such a temporary dwelling. One person's voice sounds so much like another's. It's confusing. Two much light comes in through the large front windows. You have to move. You have to speak up over and over again. You have to conclude with words that will linger, that will linger. But then you decide to continue anyway though at a different location. There is the subject that is and the subject that wants precedence. Which one will survive till the morning, which one will the parrot learn?

The inextricable complexity of this deception, fallacious and precipitant, was unavoidable. The sufferer of these perils is unknown. The only inference deduced had subdued the stubbornness of human passions, had packed away the words and carted them off across the invincible whiteness of the unlined page. At the same time you say, "are you sure?" An instance occurred which affected the majesty of the supposition. No more, slain without caution, self-expelled, perhaps suspected, taken refuge, experience had shown infinite power. Lips closed, belief shaken, deceived at an overpass, destitute of happiness, scarcely credible, this incident had terminated the wanderings, the danger of errors. You will not wonder what once had for so short a time been in a thousand cadences. You want knowledge and appear to pursue some end that the obligation to speak could not discover in its actual state. You exaggerated ideas. You and your path will be toilsome. Veracity. You have nothing which the laws permit you to call your own. You must consent to enjoy the services of the present possessor. The voice downstairs. You, be ready.

At the airport the sky seems clear as crystal. You can read the letters on the airplanes as they land. Some places seem finer then others. In the morning you had said this is your kind of place as the waitress brought the coffee. The place itself made you jovial, lighthearted, and happy in this otherwise dark time. In the bookstore you wandered for hours considering carefully each selection. You could handle no more. More coffee then and, ironically, you followed that drink with a nap before boarding the plane. Later the papers had to be signed, the calculations made, the desk cleared, one page written, and two conversations completed. It is impossible to stay at home this morning. But you have things to do elsewhere and so it is no inconvenience. Make one circle and then another. Two zeros become eight. This is the only sane lottery. This is the gold in the facade of the dwelling place. This is your life. What do you remember? Someone has punched holes in the sky and it's not just the light that you see, but it's also the sounds that you hear. The crows again, yes? And the first morning train. Above that the sky is clear, the sky is rust.

And down you go. The book crumbles, decays. The pages yellow and become brittle; so it is with you. In the end you sink back into mystery. Every single you is a glimpse of this central fact, this agony. You remain such an abundance, such a substitute. This puts an end to agony, temporarily. You have been granted so much reciprocity, so much opportunity. There has been too much cheating and this may yet ruin it. Start over again a whole series of stones and add the color orange next. Orange is a good word. The philosophers have been quite explicit about it: you cannot become it and so down you go from the glass enclosure to the open field. Hurry upstairs. Slats in shades always get out of line and it remains your responsibility to straighten them. One fingernail clicks against an other for over an hour. The stones are too large, too heavy and you can't spell the word that follows stone. You can't even imagine the following day nor recall the prior one. Whose idea was it anyway? Is the paper here? What's the weather say? All that deserves to be called you is nothing but spirit. Let the quantum-mechanical music through. You have been split. Now go.

It must be time for bigger risks, larger stakes, heretofore unimagined results. It must be time for contracts. But then you go back to your car and drive away from it all. Something invites you into the circle but you cannot recall the name and so say nothing. Everyone seems to be a regular Joe. That's the way it is. Each planet has its satellites; each sun, its planets. Just think, this is the only one you will ever know. You are reluctant to leave the room, you are afraid of the dance. The circle broadens enough to enclose you, the circle spins too fast and it becomes a noose. You cry out but cannot remember the name. You are a bad actor. You play "Louie, Louie" in a lounge over and over again. You cannot remember your lines and you know only three chords. You have huge circles under your eyes and cut your chin while shaving. You constantly lose the beat and force the rest of the band to cover your mistakes. The director asks you to do it again and again. The rest of the band likes the way you load the truck. Everyone likes the coffee you make on the set before shooting starts. The owner asks the others why they keep the guy who can't keep the beat. The editor cuts you out of the film. Once, you made a recording. You help load the truck even though you're not part of the union. You have to do something. Next time you can be a pilot, next time you can be a clown. Next time you'll start sooner, practice longer. Next time you won't take no for an answer.

Off to the side of the road a truck has jack-knifed. Traffic has backed up for miles. There is little concern for the driver. Are those vehicles that speed by on the shoulder the property of rescue workers? You'll never know. There's so much you'll never know. He has said this many times; it is one thing he does know for certain. You used to make your *f*s one way but now perhaps for a year you've been making them in a completely different way. Instead of a continuous motion of the hand, you make one *f,* lift the pen, and then make the second *f.* You do not know why you started doing this or why you continue to do so. You cannot pinpoint the exact date of when you started. Yes, there's so much you'll never know. You wanted to tell him about your *f*s, the *f*s seemed such an essential thing, such an apt example, but he sits relaxed, discussing his art. You have only the number; not the key. At night when you see the mastodons and leopards you wonder about the wisdom of such self-sacrificial election. You have created frames from the forest that surrounds your house, from the trees that you know so well. Each frame has been different from the one that preceded it, each frame has been a new challenge that offered both agony and discovery. On the other hand, he takes the same dozen elements and repeats them time after time.

Any pop song will be popular if it receives sufficient air time. Repetition, then, is the key to the house in which he lives. Keep walking.

You don't have a style. Therefore, it will be difficult to turn you into a marketable commodity or to make yourself into one. You believe that each work should be a new work. Sometimes, though, you see your work in sets of two marching hand-in-hand, double file. You don't have a style. You have a task, a goal, a project, a pace to keep, daily jogging, weekly racing to keep that pace. Has he found his formula or does he probe the essential fact, the ultimate question? And you, what do you do? What do you think you are doing? We are not through with you yet. Not by a long shot. Don't go. You can't. All the exits are guarded by trained but vicious black bears that have been imported to this country sometime before the fall of the former Soviet Union. They hate capitalists and will charge madly at the red of a Coca-Cola can. Drop sail and prepare to be boarded: your page is ours; we are in control. The race has finished and you haven't even gotten started. In the center of the circle there is a hole. It is a vacuum and soon the circle will collapse through its center taking you and your contest with it. It is a lasso, it is a noose. You are chained to your chair by your legs, your wrists, and your neck. Good luck.

He was here for four days. He tells you a number of things, a number larger than four. You've been playing. They call you "the gnat" because they can't see you and you come out of nowhere, move so fast that all of a sudden you're there stealing the ball or in someone's face as they're about to shoot the ball. All of a sudden you're down the court, you've switched channels, you've taken a book off the shelf to read "Basketball is a Holy Way to Grow Old." The cover has a hole in it. The pages crumble as you turn them. You try to write on them but they are bucking you like waves in a storm-tide. You start out one way and always turn to another direction. Is it you or this bronco busting paper? Tame it. Whip it into shape. At least leash it and take it for a walk in the park on Sunday. Clean up the mess. Use this paper to clean up the mess. Throw it out. Start over again. He was here for four days. He told you a number of things, a number larger than four. How many do you want to know?

It's easier to tell what's actually there in the writing if you've invented it than if it's something deeply familiar: one blue and white high-top sneaker, one black Swiss Army watch, one plain silver color key chain holding several keys – silver and gold. You used to dream of uncut lawns. When you drove the car the blacktop road seemed a fuzzy green color at times. This green was the coal-black color of your boot straps. The first thing you did in your new life was to measure the space for the refrigerator. Jesus called this: the resurrection. You slept all afternoon and wrestled with the cross all night. There were so many incarnations of evil spread out across the floor. You came home and slept some more. Mercy, mercy: you came home and slept some more. Jesus called this your salvation free from nightmare. The bars on the windows became slats in an open shade through which the sun shone brilliant light, a light that makes the grass grow high about the stones. One swims one day, slips and falls the next, and has a stone thereafter. Clip it. Clear it. Read the name and date, remember the walk and the sound of her voice, a falling off at the end of a line. It's been such a long, long time. It remains so familiar. It beckons.

Your spine happens to have been the pen with which you wrote this and this has left you spineless, frightened. Try writing in a different color. Try to get around – somehow – the standard black and blue. Try green again or the purple of majesty! You will not wake up a month from now, two months. You must do it now. Things come together in unexpected ways and the words that'll get you there are never entirely your own. (The more eccentric the better.) It's a child's game of wandering farther and farther into a strange neighborhood, each time returning home safely. You will certainly learn something about your habitual gestures, about the places where you give up. John says that there are many dead writers living in the present. You belong to the vocabulary of the dead. The child only wants the same story over and over again in the exact same way and so you offer look-a-like pages. Then you roll down the stairs, out the door, and into the street. It's the wrong day of the week. The car has pulled into the driveway and off to the side. There's a parrot inside that says, "Now roll down the stairs, out the door, and into the street." That's all he says, but that is a lot for him to say and as it turns out – you've said it, too.

It was one of those situations where they had to scrape the body off the road. Luckily, they were able to attach a string to the leg, to run a new one up through the hollow. That's about all that you could remember, though every once and awhile you can feel a sudden ping of pain in the back of your neck. You got up early to discuss scheduling and then went back to sleep. You could feel the wood of the chair rails in your back as you slept. You cooked early rather than late. You went in the old directions. The news had never arrived; alterations had been completed. You broke the rules and took more than your allotment. Then, once you had started, the pages turned slowly until completed. It must have been soon after that that the truck arrived. It was an iron, you were a shirt, the road was an ironing board. It went right over you, non-stick, smoothing out your creases. The garbage can filled with hangers. You won't be needing them anymore. Fold yourself neatly. Put yourself away in a drawer.

Monotony, not harmony or polyphony. Don't shoot yourself in the foot. Don't give up the store or sink the ship. The length will surprise even you. How could anyone so proceed? Do you know that the trees which have been up all night are all abroad again this morning before you? Then, turning the page, there appeared before you that circle of pure and incomparable delight. Never trust just your solitary streets. They cross the circle. Yet, don't mistake joy for luck when looking quick into the glass. The gates will not admit mistakes, only accuracies, only arrows pointed home. Make us wandering children in this world again. Curious anticipations, but as you have nothing to do but to think by day and dream by night all this begins to be discernible in a certain open flower, a tall one still in bloom by the side yard though wavering now close to the ground. Have you considered a switch from blue to red? All these phrases about houses are repetitions of other generations.

You are in a hurry, aren't you? Meet on the steps; not at the flagpole. The eye seldom shudders. Never mind. Below you there are footsteps, next to you the machine hums, in front of you there are shadows that darken the page. What is a book? If you would see the object, you must look at the object itself, and not at its shadow. Deep, deep, and still deeper and deeper you must go, if you would find out the heart and soul of it. You must interrogate it yourself, shine the light right into the hollows of each of its letters, read between the lines, in other words. Infernally black ink, white walls, and you in the middle of the room, your shadow on the right wall moving with the lines hard and bitter. Morning comes, you always loved it, the whole general inclusive hell of the same departed day. Infernally black ink summoning forth your skeleton. You don't read over the page; you don't take your eyes away from the shadow on the wall. But you do lie and cheat and steal, hide one page behind the other, recite your lines with one eye closed and the fingers of your left hand crossed behind your back.

The light isn't dying, and you're not facing disaster. It is true, though, that you can't get your mind off garbage cans; particularly a large blue one with black wheels capable of holding so many gallons. You consider carefully how best to cart it about in your car and where you would like to display it in the house. It smells like a new car but, nonetheless, you look carefully inside to be sure that there are no insects, especially since you will bring it into the house. It is a deep, beautiful blue like the ocean. It, too, can hold so many gallons. It has a top with an air hole in the center. Is this the sacred circle of which you have written? The handle sprouts out of the top where it grows widest. The handle is black like the wheels, but the handle is a blossom and the wheels are not, the wheels are hardly noticed at all. After so many days you may put the can in the center of the room. It is capable of holding so many gallons, it is capable of containing the room. It is a very capable can. It is enough of a reason to continue. You have found the rhetoric that allows this measure.

You've attached yourself to the planet, sucking on it for nutrients. You can't go it alone. It's a crowd scene, people spread across the blue canvas. You've found a spot for everything. For example, his hand on her stomach. Someone has asked you to leave sooner than was in the master plan. Around and around you go, counting. Downstairs introductions are made swiftly. It is raining. The banks cannot be reached. But you reattach yourself to the planet *just in case*. Every city is an imaginary place. Soon you are asleep, but not for long. Outside the window an animal calls out its animal cry to you. You would like to reply but are unsure of its language. Is it "t" after every "s" or "s" after every "t"? You cannot remember and it is too late to play the tapes you have in the back room. In the velvet crowd scene one woman moves, lifting herself slightly out of the water for a moment and glancing down at her breasts. This is no cause for celebration. Tomorrow you must plant the flowers in front of the house, tomorrow you must water the lawn.

You have realized the limitations of life: only so many languages, only so many places, only so many projects. Too many contracts of consent to do something for nothing, too many districts under rule. You're growing tired of hearing the word repeated. Improper, wicked projects solve no issues. Is the first ellipsis yours? More words, force, property. Splintered by an unread text, the interpretation remains incomplete, unfinished. Objects, classification, order: repetition. Make an order out of disorder: repeat the process. When his sentences ran dry, Flaubert flung himself on his divan: he called this

his "marinade." For you it is one pronoun or another; always one or another, one after the other. Repeat the ride in the box and then put the box inside a larger box and then put the ride in the box and the larger box in an even larger box. Ship it to all the cities on your list. Insure it for one-hundred dollars. (Keep in mind that you're ninety-nine percent water.) Keep in mind that you *must* arrive at the airport two hours before departure for all international flights.

If you can park the car, then you can get a room, but despite the thousands of acres everything is so compact in the center and there are no parking spaces and at this late hour everything looks shut for the night. Then you see a car load of kids get out at the tavern. They come out – tipsy – soon after with two older women, parents of some of them, perhaps, you think. There's a light on in the grocery store and you enter but are greeted by a man in a white shirt and black tie who directs you around the metal railing that separates the entrance from the exit and points you to the door. You had a chance, though, to ask him about parking and about the building across the street. He said sorry he couldn't be of any help with parking and of the building across the street he knew nothing. You got back into your car that you had left running at the curb. You looked in the rearview mirror for any signs of the police, saw nothing, and breathed a sigh of relief. You had heard that they are very strict about parking here. You know how to curse; you have learned the language. By and by you will strike, you will rub the sore.

Now choose colors. The amphitheater has a sort of gray-green look early, very early in the morning, but when the sun first hits it, it turns orange, then purple, then yellow, and then – its actual color – blue. You know this blue to be the so-called amphitheater blue. It is the blue of victory and you have had little interest in it until this time. After recalling the past all morning, after going around in circles, after dropping off the message and checking accounts, you have decided on it. What happened after the resolution you cannot remember though you are certain that some things have been mislabeled. As long as the *general category* is correct, you say with some emphasis, then you don't care. Still, the discovery makes you a little bit restless as four other possibilities circle through your head. Just as you remember to check the sheet in the left-hand file cabinet water starts to leak through the ceiling. That's it, you say, that's it.

Each reading is a layering as well as a circle that you travel and the reader follows for as long as the pages keep turning. Following you on your walk, the reader becomes aware of your habits. You do not travel alone and so the walk reveals something of the way of others – their outside shot, their speed, their tribute. You run faster on the straights to try to out distance the reader, but it is not possible. You rent a bicycle with the hope that with this extra speed the reader will give up, stop pestering you, but it does not work and finally you decide to stop messing around, to finish it once and for all, to get away and to get that much needed rest and so you take a cab to the airport, empty out your savings via electronic transfers, and board the Concorde to Paris. At Orly there are too many voices whispering and they frighten you. It is raining, everything seems too still, too black and white. In the city they await you. You get out of a cab at Saint Sulpice. Money is no object, you have lots of it now. A crowd gathers in the square and they form a circle around you.

When you close your eyes you see these faces that are speaking to you but who they are and what they are trying to say is very difficult to figure out. They are not happy and seem to warn you about something that you can't quite get. They frighten you yet you do not want to open your eyes because you know that if you do they will disappear and you do want to understand what they are trying to say, very much you do want to understand. You doubt that you will be able to recall them, to summon them again once they disappear. You have to understand. Lives are at stake. That much you do know, that much you do understand. But the faces are sad and ugly, mangled and in pain, angry and scornful, strong and certain and all of this frightens you and you begin to shiver, you begin to sweat and to shake. Still you do not understand. It seems so close, so close and you want to understand. They reach out to you. You reach out to them.

They're hitting you in the small of your back. You don't know why. The man in the moon is walking back and forth in the hallway outside your room. You read the words "no answer" as "you." First they let you fall asleep and then they shake you hard so that they wake you. This is all that they learned during the war. Or maybe they learned it from the movies and learned nothing from the war. Movies mean motion and maybe that is why they shake you and hit you. You don't know why. They're hitting you in the small of your back again. You haven't any idea why. When they finally make you stay awake you do not feel rested. The color has changed. What was once purple is now yellow. You find the color pretty. After all, you have no choice but to continue. You might as well find something pretty. You are searching, reaching for something to find. The yellow quickly disappears. You want to abide by the rules but cannot precisely remember them. You do not want to get caught cheating. You want to show some sense of independence – but well within certain guidelines. You want to have respect for others and a strong desire to work hard.

You cannot duplicate it: not the stride, not the tall flowers, not the visit nor the visitors. These are your limitations; there are no possibilities. You will take your instructions from the central office; say yes, vote no. (It's a secret.) Resistance begins in silence. Sign your name on the dotted line. You will no longer see green, but white squares cut by blue lines. It cannot be duplicated. If you remember it, put it in some other place, some other time. This is the brown time, the drying time, the dying time: smell it. It burns again. It stinks, it scratches, it kicks, it hits you in the small of your back, it wakes you up again and again. It's all so colorful, but neither green, white, nor blue. It is brown, dull brown like a flatline. The monks hold one single note for hours and then for days. This takes practice. You have joined them at their retreat, but the war has started again and so soon you must leave them. They will kick you out. Why? It is no secret. Resistance begins in silence, but does not stop there. They can cut you open if they want, they can look inside. They will not find the answer, they will not be surprised. The answer hides between two solid black circles of ink, two eyes. You place a stone on a stone.

The grace that enables you to ritualize your pain in the continuing accumulation of sentences shames the shy but curious reader who desires a brief of history, a sort of grid map, touching on all the most important aspects of your life. The truth, please, only the truth. What exactly do you look like? All of this is necessary so that the future may learn from the past. For your convenience a question sheet (with ample space for your answers) has been attached. Please begin now. There followed a peculiar feeling of being catalogued, bound and unfree. You lifted your golden head to see the unusual, the cerulean warbler that had landed in the middle of the road and then crossed to the other side. It disappeared soon after and your golden head turned vibrant red, turned to the left to reveal its profile that cast a long shadow on the streaked, efflorescent wall. Life rewards the wounded. That's why there's so much kicking and screaming in this righteous accumulation of reproductions and revenues.

They had to lift all that wood up the hill. You could not believe that they'd be able to do it and wondered why they didn't start from the other side, from the top of the hill and work the shorter distance down. People kept coming by on the narrow path, getting in the workmen's way, slowing them down, tiring them out. You thought that somehow, too, from the top of the hill the workmen would have a sort of momentum, if not right-of-way, and that the walkers and joggers would then be the ones to move to the side – what there was of it – to stop and let the workmen go by or else face their harpoons. Of course, in that time and place there were so many things that you could not understand and this is why – years later – you have decided to study that time, that place. Your sources are questionable as always: characters in failed novels, autobiographical dramas, the account books of art dealers. You would be better off working in wood, but you do not know it.

You were born in the house that bears your name: T-shaped, with an L-wing off the rear. Behind the house extends a pleasure garden lined with boxwood and terminating in an arbor of hornbeam. Sometimes a few minutes after your throat becomes so scarred that you can't make anymore sounds you take to the slamming of things something like the dying finale of the fireworks display. These are the happy times. You will not say it. You stood at the bottom of the stairs and shouted "Knife!" "Death!" There are so many things people don't say and what they do say is said to mask the unsaid. Sociologists are so busy with their questionnaires. They are wrong, but to assume so is also wrong. One woman died thinking she was the lost princess. Who is to deny this to her? Scientists are certain that she was not the lost one. What difference does it make? Yesterday you could look up and see the human-made satellite circling the planet. Who will deny that the object was there, who will deny that in her own mind she was the lost princess?

You were able to turn the noise into a kind of silence. You were able to buy many items at close out and offer them to your neighbors at substantial reductions. You made it possible to pave the walkways along the canal in red brick with granite curbs. You brought light into the dark, vacant buildings. You were a pal, a bit of a swell, a person of means and influence, a local, a sophisticate. Then the bottom fell out and kept falling. The band played in the room to three tables in front; the rest of the room was empty, a nice room, too – full of memories. You wanted to dance, but no one was in the mood, no one had passed the steps on to the young because no one wanted them to follow in their steps, just to get out and move along, to the moon and possibly beyond. Sometimes a few will return for the three o-clock tour, "A Confluence of Space and Time." Either more water or less can run through the turbine and there is a third possibility – none at all. You are looking for something to restore, to write about, to purchase, to spend money on, to sell at a profit. You just can't sit quietly and wait.

You have reached a silent place on the page. You keep writing letters, sealing envelopes, taking them to the mailbox only to discover that you have forgotten the stamps. For a moment you recall Chaplin in *The Bank* when he rips an envelope in half and then deposits it. What will happen, you wonder, if you put the envelopes in the box without stamps? Will the letters be delivered postage due? You put the envelopes in the mailbox, you walk away from the mailbox, you turn toward home, you walk back down the street enter the door go up the stairs sit at the desk reach for a pen put pen to page and pause: you have reached a silent place, you have returned to the start. This is what you looked like when you were born. There will be a thaw soon. The clocks turned back by act of Congress. None of it makes any sense. Words like "shattered" and "tomb" spin in the air, their letters cut from forms used by children learning how to print. Then there's a hammer mid-air, a hammer and a spike: up, down; up, down. The light shines right into your eyes and the good doctor asks you questions.

This is it. You have run out of time again. This time for real. You looked for a chair to sit down in but there is no time to sit down even if there were a chair somewhere nearby. You kneel and then there is an explosive sound. The horse bolts, usually so calm, and your foot gets caught in one of the stirrups. Too bad he didn't head for the field, too bad he went straight for the wall. Your head hit the wall, something more than cuts and bruises. You have run out of time. He continued on, he continued to run, he made it over the wall, he ran in circles on the other side where you used to run from first to second, from second to third, from third to home. No one ever found out what that explosive noise was that caused him to bolt and to drag you toward the wall and then straight into it and hard, very hard against it. They have set chairs in a circle and the circle slowly moves into the shape of a tear. The others sit in their chairs, the others sit in their crying, the others look at their watches, the others glance over their shoulders, the others push back their chairs.

Dogs it is, you say – two of them, something you can get a handle on, a little control over, no dirty bird or headstrong horses, no snakes. Someone has described all this nastiness in too much detail. The wind heats up the asters that grow beside the deck. Then it starts to rain again and you say – of course – cats and dogs. What is the animal of your affection? Does it feel your heat; do you feel its wetness? The flag in your yard reads "Join or Die," it is a severed snake. The plates in your corner cupboard have been stamped with the birds of Connecticut: cardinals, blue-jays, warblers, wood-peckers, etc. A live one pecks on the side of your house at just this moment. Silly bird, you say as you step outside, gather some rocks, and hurl them at the beast. The number of the beast is the total of its pecks. It's no more Mr. Nice Guy for you. This is it. This is war. It's kill or be killed. It's love it of leave it. It's let the dogs out.

You kept repeating over and over again got to see Jesus got to see Jesus got to see Jesus. Until eventually you could see Jesus in the trees outside the window of your room. You saw Jesus crucified and you reached for the phone without turning your head, without moving your eyes from Jesus on the cross, Jesus on the cross in the trees outside the window of your room and you dialed the number, you dialed 911 and said into the receiver without turning your head or moving you eyes, "Do you see Jesus? Do you see Jesus? Do you see Jesus?" Three times you asked the question and each time the dispatcher said no, no, no, but you would not quit and said this is an emergency: you must respond, you must respond to the emergency. Outside the window in the trees, look outside the window in the trees! Now do you see the crucifixion? Now do you see Jesus? But the dispatcher said – now look, you, now look, you and then hung up the phone and the machine stopped humming then and everything was quiet, too quiet. You put a needle in a haystack. This, you said, will be your alchemy of the truth. You followed the path of Muir and Appleseed, but stopped at every stack for your sacred act of transformation. You are a magician interested in things transforming and transforming things. You are an artist interested in the truth. You have travelled far. At nightfall some of the hey becomes your improvised mattress. Now there is lice in your hair and tiny little pins in your back. You lost track of where you've been and it's been just go, man, go and now there's thirty thin sticks of steel stuck into your back. Muir had his contraption for waking-up; you'll not get to sleep. So much for alchemy; so much for your poetry. True genius rakes the leaves in the backyard. Get some pliers and pull the pins from your back. Your arms are spaghetti, your brain is boiled water, your good sense went up in steam and what's left the wise will dump down the drain.

You can hold these words in your hands, you can read these pages. Seven years ago there was nothing but fickle chances, unlucky cards. Now the whole deck has been marked for success and specific plans for an outrageous increase in your income have been filed in the blue cabinets of the back room. You'll start with the floor and work up from there, a complete overhaul before the guests arrive. The t-shirts planned for the occasion had to be replaced by hats. They wanted at least one-hundred chairs outside the door in a large half-circle stretching from one end of the parking lot to another. You turned back and chose the word "exact" to be your guide for the rest of the afternoon. Everything seemed so haphazard, so inaccurate that the word "exact" had to have been the best choice that you could have made. But when you reached across the counter you conjectured for just a moment that the twenty was a counterfeit. Gather up your kit in an old brown bag and quit town for good. You, it, circle: what else have you repeated? Too much? Yes, I think so. The triumph will be some act thought likely to bring back to life the participants in the horrible slaughter, the catastrophe. The word "moral" escaped the medium divorced from feeling. Undisciplined vices and campaigns against intolerance have roused your anger. The woods are quiet. Nothing can remove the shame that is nothing more than fear, since shrewd brutes aspire to invert your government. You could not understand, everything was confusion. You talked then of new books, asked for more coffee, breathed the perfume of it. Night became the jeans you wore hidden in the corner of the star-lit room. The act had – by then – been forgotten; the triumph, no longer imagined. The words repeated, the syntax adhered to – these equaled no perfect formula averting decline. Everything remained confusion, except for the simple things: cream in coffee, no sugar. Downstairs the quiet continued, an ever lightening blanket as the sun came up clear. Caught between window and storm, a crawling insect turned over and prepared to die. You would never be able to find it again.

You: a being searching; questioning; defining a loss of contact, a form of truth – the power possessed in sound rather than sense. Every line you pass will be recognized for what it is and therefore you do not write it down: the line at the dock, the line at the market, the line at the theater, the line at the stop. How can you so exaggerate with such a hectic rhetoric? (You thought that the key word was "electric," but even electricity runs in a circuit.) You noted parallels and swore you'd restore the book to the shelf even as into the heart of a friend. So be it, these parallels. Or are they circles formed from those straight lines that bend? "Without Contraries is no progression." Don't throw out what you plan to keep. A series of lesser works provoked you to ask, "Couldn't you find some kind of occupation?" You cannot explain the stage directions to someone who exists outside the theater. You have tried to keep count most of all and that should be enough in a world where most steps fall off-beat and in the cracks. You were like me. You listen to him. You are right. You were singing. (Memory is very deceptive.) You have business to attend to. You should see some of the others. You are giving up. You must go home. (Leave me alone.) (They faced each other.) You know the news. You know what you want. You fool! Who asked you to come? You didn't know. You'll see. You were very light-hearted. You forget. You are not to be pitied. You are free. What can you expect? You know that there are souls constantly tormented. You have understood. You feel the need. You think. You gaze. You do not doubt. You are making a mistake. You frighten me. You hurt others. You know nothing, nothing. You ought to have called out long ago. You'd better listen. (It snowballs.) You pamper yourself. You should get up. Wake up. You haven't seen anything. (He looked at her strangely.) You will leave everything. You may regret it later. You must. (You know me.) You were beginning to fall. You must think it over.

The crash on Christmas Eve. At home children waiting for gifts, for you. The glasses shatter in your eyes. Their intent, to improve vision, now blinding one eye completely and the other partially. A surgeon in France says that he can restore full sight to your partially blinded eye. You will not drive and he says to avoid two things: sudden stops and chilly drafts. He warns you that "of this you must be certain." You will not fly. Agreed: the train will be best, but you are not blest. As the train speeds through the Alps an unexpected avalanche abruptly halts it. (What avalanche comes as expected? What life is not snowed under?) More follows, more of the avalanche that is your destiny. The windows break and twisted metal pins you to your seat. The wind circles the angry stone of your eyes. Blind in both eyes, you return home to your wife, to your children, to your city. You can hear the merry-makers. You can hear the celebration, the music, the laughter, the swift feet on the ancient pavement. It is the start of a new year. You join the merry-makers. You join the celebration. Resolved: you will learn to see in a new way. You sit with your left arm cupped in your right hand. Your head bowed, your feet apart. Except for you the bench is empty, except for you the park is empty, except for you the world is empty. Yesterday's papers fill the trash can, three-quarters of it. Today and tomorrow will fit in it, too. The squares of the walkway resemble the grid map of the world you thought you would see if not conquer. You were taught to remove your hat inside, but now have become so overwhelmed by circumstances that you do not understand that you have removed it and placed it at your feet here in the park, here on the walkway. You want to understand. Perhaps, the pulse of your heart beating in the veins of your arm will tell you something. Quick now, turn your head toward its rhythm. What do you hear? Have you proven to yourself that you are still alive? To one side the shadow of the shrubs cuts across the bench where you sit and to the other side sits the garbage can still only three-quarters full. Fill it and put someone back to work. Stop complaining. Fill it and rejoin society.

Everything in squares. The paved lot; the unpaved lot. A path between them, connecting them. Paint hurled at the stone dripped down from two skeletal eyes. Stayed that way – still as stone. Others toppled over – remained that way. The entrance to the trail unmarked, unkept. But the stones visible nonetheless. Surprise stuck in the throat and stayed there. The lot built on top of the dump. Brambles, some trees, and the stones in the unpaved lot. The message unclear, the origin uncertain. The eyes sunk in their sockets, the paint becomes tears. Everything gray: the brambles, the lots, the stones, even the surprise. Gray surprise, not red or lavender. Nothing separates the lots but their edges: no cut and soaked lots, no curbs poured in cement. A road and a rodent on it. What is the connection? Beneath the brambles are the names. Perhaps, some other information, but not enough information to understand, not enough information to know their true names. Nothing in the paved lot except pavement. Only thing in the unpaved lot besides brambles and some trees: you, the rodent, and the stones.

You sit here thinking of there. The towers of damp brown boxes confront you, the smell of insecticide repulses you. The barren walls surround you with their emptiness. You have seen remodeled rooms with blue curtains instead of brittle shades; with ornamented columns instead of cardboard towers tilting, collapsing into the worn rug centered just so. You have tried the magician's trick, but still it remains out of fashion, out of ideas, out of use. The notice has been posted, the lights shut, the door locked – you have left it for scavengers, for the insects that will arrive after the insecticide has dissipated. You have already dissipated. You will not consider decoration. You will not prop-up the sinking economy with luxuriant spending. Someone says step back and take a look at it and you say what's wrong with it. One rug has a design on it; one rug is gray. Yet, both are rugs. You sit here thinking of there, of opening the door, of turning on the light, of looking at the walls, of moving the boxes, of burning the furniture, of breaking through on one side, of doubling the size.

The cat has a rodent caught in its paws. The cat lets the rodent go. The cat pounces on the rodent and with a sudden movement of its head, a sudden bite of its teeth the cat rips a long, trembling vein from the pinned down rodent's neck. The cat moves away slightly, the vein half in its mouth; half in a paw, the vein still pulsing with life like an infant snake or a minnow beaten in the tide, beached. The rodent shakes, too, close to its death, it gasps, but cannot breathe, cannot speak. Still it utters an awful, plaintive silent cry. You walk by and see the rodent dying at your feet and see the cat eating and playing with an animated string. You move closer to the cat, closer also to your wife. The cat looks at you and looks away. Your wife turns and you move closer. The rodent has died, the cat has gone home, has gone next door, the rain has stopped, the vein has become a cello's string that the cellist plays pizzicato and your wife, she stretches and sings.

It was not possible to attend the reading. It seems a missed opportunity, though in one trip – in one lifetime – it is not possible to do everything. A disagreement and a train missed, a walk by the University, the old buildings, a new district for you – so quiet at this hour. Cold, but warm enough if you keep moving, if you keep rubbing your hands together. The station suffices for toilet and sink, though you can't keep tipping the attendant if you intend to drink a coffee – hot – later. Along the back of the antiquities museum there's a large open garden with benches along its sides. At the other end of it and across a narrow street an even narrower drive leads to the courtyard of one of the few official dormitories. No one stirs at this hour, not even those involved in this district's well-known sex trade. What an interesting hour of the day, you think, there is no other like it! Enough is enough, though, you decide, and retrace your steps to the genteel neighborhood in which you live. At the top of the stairs – dukes up – you continue the fight.

At the top of the stairs: the square. At the top of the stairs: the circle. Combat begins between circle and square at the top of the stairs. The chairs are in place; the chairs are out of place. A matter of perspective, of opinion, not fact. Not to be recalled, the morning or the night. How old are you? How old are you in dog years? Not to be recalled, what happened. In the street, in the middle of the street in the busiest part of the city: "this is the end." But at night, at the top of the stairs what happened there? How old is she? Is the other dancer her daughter; will she set her daughter free; will she chain her daughter to the ladder, chain her daughter to the ladder and tell her to look down, to fall down, to drop down upon her knees, to roll on her side, to roll on her side and stretch her arms out in front of her as far as the chains will allow her to stretch them? It is very bright for a moment by the door. Everyone wears a different hat and new shoes. Everyone will shout, shout, shout. They will shout at the top of the stairs, at the very top of the stairs.

You can go from the weight room to the swimming pool, but you, you with the red hair, you must first lift the weight from your body, the weight that weighs more than your body, the weight that crushes your body, the weight that has been crushing you for eighteen years. You cannot write down the number three times each day. You cannot unlock the door, not without the number. They have polished the floor for you. They have put mirrors on the walls for you. You see yourself and complain of the repetition. You see yourself and feel pain in your hands from holding the weight, the terrible weight above you. This is where it ends, you say and then remember that those are words from the book that they held in the mirror in front of you. Those are their words. You can hear splashing in the pool. Next thing you know you are on a mountain top. This cannot be explained and you do not try to explain it. You let it go. Arms extended, way up on your toes you breathe in the air. It is delightful. It is delicious.

You agreed that you like the song, too. "It's so cold in Alaska." And then when he wanted to come into the house – knowing full well that he would want to see every room and that his boots had been in the mud that day – you did not object. On the way you picked up a syringe, carried it for awhile until you found a garbage can, and then got rid of it. You didn't want to walk into the house with that thing. When you passed your friend's house you could see – even from the end of the driveway – that he had gone to the concert. "It's so cold in Alaska." At your house he *did* go into every room. Later at the zoo an obnoxious boy kept pulling the tail of an owl, pulling it down and making it roll up like a party favor. You asked him to stop. He wouldn't and then you nudged him a little with your hand and said, "Hey, stop it." You wondered how anyone could be so weird. Then the little pudge ball turned around and punched you after he had turned around and exclaimed in amazement "You hit me" and you said "Go ahead hit me" – anything, any ploy to get him to stop bothering that owl.

Then his father came over. The boy told his father that you had hit him. You tried to speak calmly and rationally to the father, said that the boy kept pulling the owl's tail, said yes, I said "Hey" and nudged him, you know what I mean. The father got the park police. Several witnesses stepped forward to say that they had seen the boy pulling on the owl's tail. At the top of the stairs near the owl's perch there wasn't enough room for all these people, all this interrogation. You had no idea that the day, any day would turn out this way. The park police took you to a room and while you waited for the town police you once again explained what happened – slowly, carefully, and in detail. The local police came and arrested you and told you to get a lawyer. When your lawyer arrived once again you explained what had happened – slowly, carefully, and in detail over and over again. You spoke calmly and rationally. The lawyer said that both sides have their witnesses; quite frankly, he said, it's a tossup. Then he added after a pause – and all the owl will say is who! who!

Push, He Said. Pull, He Said.

I WAS IN A CLASS taught by the poet Robert Creeley. He was a good teacher, but sometimes I got the sense that he was stuck in another time or that – despite his fame as a poet – the world had passed him by. Certain phrases he'd repeat all the time. Perhaps, that's poetry, but it sure isn't prose. He'd say "he had a certain disposition" or "I then became aware of" and these commonplaces would send him off on a monologue of undetermined duration. I must make it clear right here, right now that I loved to listen to his stories that each were tens of minutes longer than any of his poems. It was in his class that I decided on a career as a chiropractor.

I'm not sure how I reached my decision, something about a correspondence between the bones of a person and a person's words and that I was so overwhelmed by the poet's voice I knew I could never repair anyone's words and therefore I chose second best: bones.

The funny thing is that somehow – it's too long a story to tell here – I ended up as the only chiropractor in the town of Waldboro, Maine. I do a lot of work for the athletic department at the small state college two towns away. Notice the implied transition, the implied connection: college / college. I said I had little hope at being any good as a writer. But, I have become an excellent chiropractor. And this is the amazing thing: my old professor is now my patient.

You see, he has a summer place here in town not too far distant from my office. He is sick now and I provide what relief I can. I assuage his weary bones. He hardly speaks at all now. It is so difficult for him now to utter a single word. Each word gets caught somewhere deep in his body and his sickness won't let him get it out. He becomes silent and I can see how sad he is then. Words were his life.

Every so often though through pushing here and pulling there, by applying the right pressure at just the right place I can get him to squeak a little. When he does this he sounds just like a bird, a bird in song, a bird in flight. He squeaks "bob white, bob white."

It wasn't until after he left for the winter that while reading a book of his he left for me I realized that his full name is Robert White Creeley. I didn't know that. That surprised me. There it was inside the front cover. Title page verso. I knew then that it was his own name that he tried so hard to eke out on those days when I pushed and pulled and applied just the right amount of pressure. "Bob White," he'd squeak and, yes, that was a smile on his face at those times, a soaring smile that stretched its wings from cheek to cheek.

Adam and Eve

LUCY TOLD ME that the world began with Eve's plum and not with Adam's apple and that these people who lived in this terrible place entered paradise when Eve got Adam to bite the plum after a dove had flown overhead that told Eve to get Adam to bite her plum. I knew she had it all wrong and told her so, but she wouldn't believe me. She never does.

Soon after this we started fighting. I don't know why. But I felt like the bottom had fallen out, like I was walking on quicksand, like it was the end. She hung up the phone on me. All this because of one fruit or another. Like, who cares?

So I wrote to her to tell her that I didn't care, that any fruit is fine with me. Whatever she likes, you know. I sent her a gift basket of fruit, too. A sort of humorous way – I thought – of making up, of telling her so. But it didn't work. A week or two later I got the basket back – rotten fruit included. There are so many things I can't figure out.

Like the keys. What do the keys have to do with any of this, I wondered? I mean if it's over, if I've been expelled from the Eden of her company and cast out into the cruel world of solitude, then why hasn't she asked for her keys back? Is it a test? Do I dare let myself in to her apartment one day at a non-threatening time like 5:00 and set the table with flowers, wine, and food – no fruit, though, right? I know, I should just mail them back to her and you'll say I'm a creep because I don't but you don't know anything. You don't know that I know that she knows that I have her keys.

We're all fools. You see, it's too late for keys, for apples or plums.

Everything but my heart has turned to rot. My heart is stone, stone, marble cold stone. There it was this morning in the paper, second section, second to last page: Lucy Evans Thorngold, 37, Fifth Victim of Tainted Cider.

So she was right all along. It's plums, not apples.

To Catch The Nearest Way

"So," he said.

And then she said, "I don't think so."

He replied with some anguish, "please."

"No," she said firmly. "Absolutely not."

"Well, why not?" He asked plaintively.

"Because," she said flatly, matter of factly. And then she added before he could say anything. "I know. 'Because why?' 'Why not?'" She imitated him and then slowly, authoritatively demanded, "Don't whine."

"I'm not whining," he said yet there was that plaintiveness, that defensiveness in his voice again.

"But you would have if I gave you the chance," she noted with certainty. "You're always whining lately," she added.

"No, I'm not," he noted emphasizing the word "not."

"See. There you go. Whining." Her words were concise, clipped to the mark. "And now you won't say anything." She moved her head mockingly as she said this, moved her head as if to say "poor baby."

"Why should I? You'll just say that I'm whining again." He seemed to speak with complete despair, certainly discomfort.

She gave in a little bit. "I'm not going to say anything."

"Oh, so now you're the one not speaking." He spoke these words with a feeling of one-upmanship. It was, however, short-lived.

"That's not what I meant," she said. "I meant that I'm not going to accuse you of whining as soon as you start to speak."

"That's a relief," he sighed.

But she added very quickly and with some visible amusement, "I'll wait to see what you have to say and then decide."

"Quit it," he implored her.

"Quit what?" She mocked him, playing innocent.

"Being such a wise guy." He was whining.

"Who me?" And she did indeed mock him.

"This tent is too small for this shit." He was frustrated, exasperated, and beginning to get angry.

"Well most of it is yours." She was victorious.

"That's not what I meant." He was defeated.

But she continued, "Whoever heard of bringing a flute camping? And a pipe? Rustic, but pretty idiotic – unless you thought you'd keep the mosquitoes away. Keep the mosquitoes away with the pipe smoke and speak to the pretty little birds with the flute song." She said this with a sarcastic lilt and then she shifted to false enthusiasm and put much emphasis on the last word (his name) of her next sentence. "Good idea, Bert."

"Are you through?" He asked annoyed. "Have you talked yourself out for the night? Can we go to sleep now?"

"What? No nookey!" She said. He couldn't tell whether she spoke sweetly or flirtatiously, coquettishly.

"Elissa," he sighed and that was all. For his frustration grew.

"What Bert, dear?" She mocked him again.

"You're a pain." He didn't know what else to say and what he said was neither very clever nor very meaningful.

"No pleasure?" She asked seductively, rubbing her fingertips across his cheek. Then, once more, she abruptly shifted her tone. "Are you too tired tonight, honey? Hard day at the office? Students out of control? General Van Etren on your back? The weight of the world a burden on your shoulders. God ..."

"Oĸ. Elissa," he interrupted her. "Enough already."

"Not until you say 'uncle.'" This wasn't a request. It was a command.

He replied, "Oh, Christ."

"Bert!" she said feigning shock. "I am surprised. That's so extreme for you, so out of control, so totally random." It seemed she could continue this list indefinitely. But Bert implored once more, "Can't we just go to sleep?"

"Why?" she asked. Then she commanded him again in two sharp, steeled words: "Don't whine."

"What?" he asked still a bit bewildered by everything.

"You're whining again, Bert." Now she was annoyed, but playfully altered her tone to a new mockish style as she assumed the timber of a man's voice and said, "Be a man! Here, take your medicine. Step forward lad and volunteer. The Queen needs you in her army."

"Elissa." He was exasperated.

"Bert." She did mock him. She placed her palm on his cheek and struggled to contain her laughter.

"There are too many people around in this campground." He said this without looking at her, but while looking off into nowhere instead.

"No," she said softly, almost whispering. Her words all of a sudden had become kisses, foreplay. "There's just you. Just me. No one else in the world. The universe. Just us. Just Bert and Elissa. Bert and Elissa."

"So?" he asked.

The Monument Watcher

"WHO'S YOUR ROOMMATE? I've never seen him."

"Oh, yes. You have. He's the monument watcher. Everybody has seen him."

"What's he do?"

"Take care of it, I guess. I don't know. I never see him. He won't last long here. He hasn't been to a class the whole term."

"What is this stuff. Yours?"

"His."

"What's he do with this stuff?"

"Gives it away."

"Who takes it?"

"No one. I guess that's why it's still here."

"How did you get stuck with him?"

"The lottery."

"Well, you won't have to worry about that next year."

"No, I won't."

"Did you ever ask him why he does it?"

"Did you?"

"No."

"I did. Once early in September I asked him exactly what it was he was trying to accomplish. He asked me if I had ever seen *The Day The Earth Stood Still.* You know, the one with Klaatu and Gort?"

"Yeah. I've seen it."

"Well, then he went on real serious and said it wasn't Gort anyway but Lock Martin and that that doesn't make any difference. He asked me if I understood."

"What did you say?"

"I said yes, of course, I understood. What do you think I'd say? Then he asked me if I remembered the end of the movie and again I said yes. And he said remember at the end how the soldiers kill Klaatu and Patricia Neal has to get back to Gort and tell him Klaatu's message?"

"What message?"

"The one Klaatu made her memorize before he got shot! Barada nikto and all that. Then he told me to think of this: what if she got back to where Gort was and she was too afraid to speak?"

"Deep."

"I know."

"And then what?"

"And then he said no more as if that explained all his actions. He went back to planting his flowers or whatever as if I wasn't even there. I stood there waiting for the rest of the story or some sort of explanation or something. But nothing. Silence. I didn't say anything either. I mean this nut is my roommate!"

"So, what did you do?"

"I left."

But now it was spring. No one tried to break through to him anymore. They left him alone with his granite slab. It bore the inscription of five names and one date. He kept it clean. Around it, he planted flowers by day and lit candles by night. Day in and day out, he was there before all the others awoke and after all the others went to sleep. It had started near the end of the first week of his first semester. Now it was spring. He was still there, busy now more than ever: planting and pruning, sweeping and cleaning, and, seemingly, praying, too.

All this changed rather suddenly. One day shortly before dawn, several trucks pulled into the campus lot nearest the monument. From the trucks the drivers unloaded the equipment, a spider's web of wires. They prepared to shoot a segment for a weekend news show. The television journalist arrived and then the pace of events quickened. They had come to the campus this spring to film the monument and the monument watcher.

The journalist read a prepared script off a prompter as the cameras captured every name on the slab and paused at the date. This segment was to be shown on the tenth anniversary of the event that the granite marker commemorated.

Next, they brought the watcher into the picture. The journalist mentioned how it was his first year and how all this year he had maintained the monument in its present splendor, more splendid, in fact, than it ever had been before. Then the journalist turned toward the watcher to ask him some questions. But he did not speak. He did not say a single word.

Later that month he was seen taking his exams. He would return the following fall to live in a room of his own choosing.

All That There Is Between Us: The Time Capsule

WHEN THE OTHERS tried to follow me in their cars they got lost because I made so many turns. I returned to the highway, pushed the pedal hard and my vehicle, it flew. We met up again much later at the south end bar. "The waiters circulated like ghosts in the midst of a fog of triple origin: human, alcoholic, nicotinic," Queneau had written in his *Last Days*. I looked at my friends and saw that I sat with two skeletons, two mere skeletons. I looked at my hand and saw only bone. The building itself was just a frame and the wind blew through it, through me, through my friends. I had forgotten to lock the door when I left and now everything was gone, everything, except the car and the highway and the directions for getting from here to there pasted on the windshield.

At that point I weighed no more nor no less than a very strong gust of wind. Then my destiny spoke to me. The world has too many slats through which light moves at odd angles, shadowing all that should be clear to me. The world has too many frames in which the light gets trapped and burns its hieroglyphic marks, but the marks cannot be read. The wind that is my body touches these burns, cools them too soon so that when I look through the slats that remain my only eyes there is only smoke curling, drifting away. This is my destiny. And when it rains, what happens when it rains, you ask? Things slow down. Ashes placed in a scale weigh nothing and so nothing happens. A trail through the woods gets changed somewhere by someone because of all that mud. Where I step no footprint remains. Yet it seems as if somewhere at sometime something did occur before it all washed away and rolled off this spinning globe.

I am a tin foil tiger, an Adirondack stick figure, a fossilized clump of earth who looks to the other side for answers, to the neighbors for sugar, to my brother for blood. I'll make my list now for no list will be possible in the next century. Everyone will be eating cassava. I read about all of this in the paper this morning. A German company wants to buy an American company; a New York radio conglomerate wants to buy a Waterbury station. Yet, all of this will take so much time. Approvals will be needed from various committees: law and order must be maintained. I've been told not to blame the organizers if I twist an ankle or end up in the woods. It's not the woods, they tell me, but the words and hence the world that confuses me.

Outside on the street people walk by or they ride their bikes. I can hear their feet. I can hear their bells. Occasionally a car goes by, always in the same direction though not always at the same speed. I can see out the windows, but not to the street below. The windows are high up and all I can see is the office building across the way. In the morning people arrive; in the late afternoon, they leave. From where I sit I can see only their heads, never the bodies to which I assume they're attached. How can I be sure of anything, after all? When I look up, which I seldom do, the ceiling greets me with its finality; its unceasing presence that unnerves me with its white constancy. If I could I would lift myself up and throw an apple or a pear at it so that there might be something up there beside that unbroken field of white, but this I can't do and so I think about the windows and they return me to the walls, always to the walls, the walls which are orange, the walls which surround me with their quiet pastoral scenes of cows and hillsides. I have thought of drilling a hole in one wall to see what's on the other side, to locate the source of that pleasant music that I sometimes hear.

One visitor referred to the whole structure as beset by faded elegance. Where he saw diminishment I look and see the stars that foretell my destiny in this time, in this place. Everything sparkles. The furniture came from a different era, descended to the present generation as a gift from a past one, one that rode about the waves in ships little sturdier than that tiger maple stand in the corner. I want to speak only of its grandeur. How from this room others had set out to reach the furtherest corners of the world. There are stars of masonry on the ceiling above and so too there are stars outside in the sky at night. If you look closely you'll see that they're not as far away as you think, you'll see that with a little more exercise, a little more study, and a proper diet we'll all be able to reach them soon. Except that pessimistic visitor – will we leave him behind, set in a sofa with hands as well as feet and instruct the living sofa to hold him there for all eternity? He will only be able to see the office building across the street, the heads bent silently to their tasks. He will see them arrive in the morning and leave in the late afternoon. He will remain and never go. He will remain and never go.

I am the master who lets snow whitewash a world of desperate lies. I am the satisfied one, happy to shoot the buzzards or erase the poem. I am the one with the hands able to lift the lines up to lips swollen with thirst, ready to speak. The oasis is not quite there. It too is an illusion or maybe it is what the blind see when they look at the sun. These lines that I cook up for the starved have little flavor or light. The hungry grow dissatisfied and impatient with the poem that is yet-to-be. They are very dissatisfied birds, these parched ones. They do not like how it feels. They do not like how it tastes. They land, approach, and pick at the dark with their talons and beaks. They fly up and swoop down again. They do not like what they see. The sand of this page is a mirror and their shadow upon it is seen by them to be their own reflection. These buzzards fly above the sand that attracts them. Come closer little birds. This ground is on fire. Be patient. Wait a little longer while I stare in the mirror at the flames that jut from just that place that used to be my eyes.

Why is it only in the mirror that I see the lines inscribed on my body? What else do I see emanating from this prophetic panel of polished glass? In the upper right hand corner in the drying, dying fog I see the initials of my first girlfriend's name. In the steam swirling toward the vent I read a message from my long departed mom. It warns me to be careful, to be wary, but of what? The answers can never be deciphered until too late. Outside the window a jet's exhaust stream streaks the sky and this too is a sign that I must read. I take out my telescope and point it toward the fading moon. It seems to wink at me – or do I blink when moving away from the eyepiece? Do I stammer when speaking on the phone, trip when ascending the stairs, take too long to re-tie my shoes? These are the lines that lead from my body to the world; these are the lines of sight. Sometimes they reveal; other times they conceal. Occasionally it is possible to tell which is which and what's what, occasionally it is possible to perpetuate oneself for another twenty-four hours or so before returning to that awful gaze in the mirror splotched with red and shadowed.

I have added a new opening chapter. I have also enlarged the discussion of this subject. I have added some new material. I have omitted some passages which I now find misleading. I retain a sense of debt to those who first helped me. I have come to appreciate all who think about the free gift in a thousand envelopes. I live. And from whom I was formed, the social order, I conceive relationships held in my mind. So far as I am aware, the actual words remain under the control of the state. Acts are another matter entirely. If I want, I borrow, manage, assist, endeavor and see what it will do to unsnarl knotty problems. In that I have not been led to such a place where I might meet a different social status, I resolve to stay at home till spring. In this matter I doubt not my sense of advantage. In the case of a testament, all efforts can be settled in the letters of the heart. I must be pardoned.

I try to step back, if not out. It doesn't work. The rampant lion on the rook pushes me back into the center where I get bloodied again and again. So we go to church for wisdom, but receive only prayers. The center is everywhere you don't want it to be. It doesn't matter. And that is why I punched you right between the eyes, that is why I bloodied your nose, that is why the referee raised my hand and not yours.

You see, that voice you heard as a child was your own. That voice called to you from the basement, from the bottom of the stairs, the dark. It spoke a language only you understood. Once it told you to jump off the stairs and another time it asked you how anyone could be so stupid and said that stupid people shouldn't be allowed to live and then you cut yourself, two little incisions behind the left ear. Stupid little person. I did not know any of this for many years. Once, while walking in the country, we listened for that voice. I couldn't hear it. I heard the birds sing and saw the sun glisten behind the pine trees. "A million dollar view," I called it. You missed it, stood shaking, looking down at your finger, listening intently to I don't know what in your dark and dissonant world. I wanted to skip for joy in the brilliancy of the world, but couldn't because there you stood next to me, oblivious to all that is beautiful in the world, intent on all that is horrible and in despair, almost dying. How could I skip then for joy? How could I leap in to the heart of it all when you chained me to the ground, took me so quick from the hilltop to your dark and damp basement?

So, you began almost every sentence with "so." So what? So I joined the Navy. Sailed about in a submarine, a barber always on staff – just like the President! "Few things are sadder than the truly monstrous," Nathaniel West wrote in *The Day of the Locust*, the first page of which is like a front door. Perhaps it is ornamented. The last page is like the back door. Those who know West well use it. Is it wood or is it stone? Is it a single word or the entire world? Is it spoken in opposition or confusion? Ships rock in that picture that's for sale. Just ask the author of all those mysteries who won the prize, took it out to the farm, and buried it along with several tapes of The Beatles singing "She Loves You" in various languages. She offered her package to the future as her own special time capsule. I left that evening earlier than usual because so many things turned out different than I had expected them to turn out. It was so early, in fact, that we thought the clocks must have stopped and compared their time to our wristwatches. The same. It was that early and that was that. We'd have to wait a bit longer to see if the future would arrive, to see if any of its occupants would want to dig up her time capsule and if they did so, what sense they'd make of it.

I have tried to change the world, but the drone of the planes keeps getting in the way. Take my word for it. This is a hospital and the television doesn't work and the food stinks and the toilet won't flush and the gardens are full of weeds. Thank God for this poem. It is all that there is between us. I have nailed it down, at last, so that the fan will not blow it away. I began it on my birthday and have titled it "The Crucifixion." Now it is in every room, nailed above the door. You must read it on your way out. That is, you must read it if you want to leave. So few do, you know. And that my friend explains the problem with the gardens. So many weeds, so few workers. So many planes in the air, circling and circling. When I think back on it, all I can remember is dancing and dancing.

All forms of communication are easily separable from problems of duration. Let us suppose that at one extreme this substance possesses a structure instead of a fortuitous solution. Genius is no man-made thing. It puts forth ideas and objects in all the materials that are worked by hands. The ancient division that both share even in this time needs a complex, crisscrossed intention to yield a finer scale. It exists rather generally for the sake of one's own initial technique. We are now events, but a graph by the same token works in perpetuation of its own signal. That will spare us the evidence closest to the premises underlying the sequence set forth here. The first to note this sequence in terms of his situation was a pilgrim, a tourist. Still, the mass reality of any innovation encountered always corresponds to a chain of prior events in the sense that most investigations can be treated as needs and things. The new behavior, the efficacy of language, the propagation of things can be treated as the amalgamation of thought that we understand in apparent remoteness from the simple confrontations every society becomes aware of merely in noting the lack of correspondence.

Beyond use, beautiful form is a function of repetition, a total adjustment; by definition, a time of a disintegrating *one*. Thus, everything corresponds to extension. When people doubt, when the visible alone is beautiful it is not easy to know the obvious. The burdensome trace of rare elements, the terrain of little use, the vein or how it came to be are sketchy, known only by deduction, if at all. We would annex the archaeological in human affairs to envisage the essence of our present. Consider hagiography or connoisseurship. What will they leave you with in the last instant of this century? I have been asked to speak about style, but have taken detours into supposition and metaphysics. In the final analysis all of what has been said leads back to a more popular topic: love. Love, that is, or the absence of it. This is a carefully reasoned conclusion, the result of much study, as much as if to say that fiction is a fact, as much as if to say many fields are open to study – reformulate them as you speak.

This sentence can be made more precise. Yet, these sentences connect memories to the place that evokes them. They describe. They move back and forth in time. They use art for quiet surprise and mix the particular with the events of the world. There is loss, but also continuation without the accumulation of display. We would annex the archaeological if it could guarantee survival past the end, past the imposition of the governors who rule without exception, unchecked. We are in the heart of the elephant to the south of you, Canada, speaking out against hypocrisy as best we can. I didn't vote for this, any of it. My friend, you sounded so tired on the phone, so tired and worn out, and yet you spoke of a new burst of energy after the morning appointment with the acupuncturist. There is something jabbing at my little toe. I can't see it. And when I remove my shoe I can't feel anything wrong with my toe or my shoe. But it does look swollen to me. It does look too pinkish, if not red and inflamed. Is it broken? Is it the start of a chaos that cannot yet be described or defined because it cannot yet be named? Is it the end? Can someone else be more precise in her words or touch?

The Tip of My Tongue

I REMEMBER THE SONG that you sang then and the words that you couldn't ever quite recall as if the fourth line always got caught on your lips and that threw you off pitch, off line right out of the song. Now I know the words, but you would sing just those few lines: "Don't you know little fool you can't win. Wake up to reality. Use your mentality." I remember the missing lines. The missing links of our lives remain. I remember the last trip and the fulfillment at least of being there, that wish, after all those years of wanting to be there. I remember the hotel restaurant downstairs. That was as far as we got, that was the sum total of a last vacation: without sun, without waves, without sights to see other than the four corners of a room, the dim light of a near-empty banquet hall. I remember "Celebrate" played constantly, every time we went down the stairs to eat: "celebrate good times, come on." Our last adventure, a walk from a bed to a table and on the return voyage after every meal, I remember you'd surmount the final stair breathless yet diligently, stubbornly continue to your room. You Puritan, you. You Northern soul. I remember. I remember you still. All that was outside awaited one of us, but it was thwarted by all that we held inside ourselves; not repression – not then, not there: love. You were not to be left, not even to see all the wonders that there were outside. I remember the words spoken, the words about gifts, about breath, about framed images. I remember so that I will not forget. I remember the color blue. I remember my white bicycle and you standing by it and me without a shirt; you in a blue checkered blouse, in the background the brown shakes of the house, the lime green of the grass, the ash gray of the patio cracked along one corner. There we stood. "Say, 'Pizza!'" I remember. "Don't you know little fool you can't win …". I've yet to wake up to reality. Remind me if you can to wake up, to watch out, to get on the right track. Remind me to be careful not reckless as I glide on my white bicycle across three lanes in a rush to meet you, to greet you, to join you, perhaps, at least, in a final breath of my own to speak one last time your name. What would I remember then? Wake up to reality? I remember I'd say nothing to you in the car during those mornings I drove you to work. Grumpy and groggy and still and silent, my legs moved separately from my body as if some other's, as if a robot's, and my arms moved but to shift the car and only the right one moved, the left remained glued to the wheel like a race car driver's. I never glanced in your direction, never smiled or offered a song to you in your honor. I just wanted to get you out of my car and quick. And so what we remember must be what falsehoods we make out of the dark forest that is lost time. You see, I shift here from the singular to the plural to cast off guilt, to locate myself in present time as Mr. Nice Guy, as a swell and pleasant son.

At Noon

AT NOON THEY WALKED. They walked from their rooms to the garden through the garden and back to their rooms. Every day. On rainy days they sat on borrowed chairs in a paneled lounge and watched television and watched television or walked through the garden and back to their rooms depending on sun or rain until they were called from their rooms or from their chairs to lunch. Called to lunch they would almost all respond to that call. They would all respond except for those few who no longer wished to eat because they no longer wished to live. Those few were like the rain, a bad day, a bad lunch. Those few were bad news in an otherwise tolerable world. The others still sparkled through memory of what they had once been. The few had forgotten even the memory of what once was. The others at lunch sat at common tables and engaged in common talk. Some men even flirted with some women. Some women even flirted with some men. Some had once been bankers and others tailors. Now all that didn't matter. Now it was their children's money that kept them there but once there all that didn't matter because for the few years, months, weeks of life they had left to live they had entered a classless society. Around a table sat men and women together conversing. There towards the large glass window, his back towards the window sat Mr. Richards talking, laughing. His thin hands, veins protruding, held an apple. Out of the pocket of the old sport coat that he wore every day now whether cold or warm, whether grandchildren brought him new sweaters or new sport coats, offerings to which he would reply, "You take it. Your wear it" – out of his pocket he took his pocket knife and slowly peeled the apple. One hand turned the apple sure and careful as the other hand held the knife that peeled it. The apple peeled, he ate it.

After lunch, Mr. Richards liked to walk by himself through the garden. He remembered. As long as he retained the memory of what he once was, he thought, there was still enough reason to live and with reason to live it would be impossible to die. The memory need not be and indeed was not the grand moments that the competent biographer would be certain to note. The life-sustaining memories were those the biographer would never know. He walked in the garden. He remembered flowers, planting flowers, not an escape from a war-time prison camp. He remembered that he did not want to be where he now was. He remembered he must not become accustomed to it.

Yet, even here the days passed quickly, too quickly and more quickly with each passing day. He reasoned, at eight months a month is one-eighth of a child's life while at eighty a year is but one-eightieth of a man's life. How quick and inconsequential a day becomes. Tomorrow and tomorrow.

The dawn of a new day, its promise still believed, he would rise zestful every day. He would not be defeated. He who in his own little way had defeated an entire nation gone mad. He believed he had a new task to accomplish, a new little way to see to its end for the nation he had adopted and which had so warmly adopted him was mimicking a madness not to be repeated.

Because he spoke openly of his beliefs his own children and grandchildren sent him here and kept him here. It is not so very hard to believe. When youth and a standardized sense of the beautiful prevail as the prized model for all, is it unreasonable to assume an undesirable dandelion should be, must be removed from the thousand blades of a green grass lawn? The distinctiveness of his features, the unique curls of skin on his forehead, the indentations across his lower lip, the eyes sunken deep into his skull as if he were already a skeleton about the wood-framed, box-shaped house were held against him for on the after shave, eyeliner scale of beauty he fared poorly indeed. He mumbled Marx. That was intolerable. He peed on the circumference of the toilet bowl never failing to never hit center.

If one took the time to listen though, to concentrate on the oddly shaped sounds of his heavily accented idiolect one would hear a voice of reason in an otherwise irrational world. A cry in the wilderness of age, he'd warn against forsaking all alternatives. He was no wheelchair revolutionary. He simply wanted ideas to be given voice for when there is only one idea constantly heard and heard again there can be no idea of what life is and how valuable it is – so he said. Redundancy cheapens. He would become annoyed, look at his grandson's face and say, "no more."

Some days they would bring the dog with them much to the attendants' chagrin. The dumb looking, lovable creature was called Butterfingers precisely for the meaning that such a moniker implies. Butterfingers was an accident prone, clumsy dog whose tail would constantly wag its way into china cabinets or a cucumber dip in a crystal bowl atop a coffee table. Saying hello to this dog posed for the majority of the humans who came into contact with him a morally significant struggle. The grandfather had a special fondness for this dog who to him had a hero's courage. The grandfather would laugh and smile with the dog. He, too, would wag his tail as it were, but here he could wag it into no trouble. No trouble. Rarely would they visit him and rarer still were their visits marked by the presence of the dog. Some days they would bring the dog, but usually not. And that word "not" seemed forever to the attendants' delight.

After lunch he walked through the garden. After his walk, he returned inside. There were many people watching television. He tried to talk to some of them occasionally and usually he failed. He used to talk to one woman in particular, but she had died.

One day when he awoke early a stout young attendant entered his room smiling and, while the old man wiped away the frost from his window, the attendant told him that it was his birthday and he wished him a happy birthday. Mr. Richards said nothing. He was rather surprised. He had no birth certificate and had long ago forgotten when his birthday was. He had not so much forgotten as he had stopped caring. He knew it was sometime in October, could count the years, was glad to be alive, why fiddle over days. "Days become years," he would think and then say to himself, "See, too much worry over the moment keeps us always separate from our lives and what should be the larger concerns of our lives. In our worry we forget." His children and grandchildren would be coming this afternoon. How else would the attendant know that it was his birthday and why else would the attendant have entered his room smiling this morning. All knew he needed no help rising, shaving, or dressing. Although sometimes he would greet an attendant or even a doctor by rubbing their chin with one hand or both their cheeks with both his hands and saying, "You get such a smooth shave. How do you do it? You must show me sometime. Perhaps, it's my razor, no?" He would never wait for or expect an answer but would invariably add his humorous maxim, "Shaving: someday I'll get the knack of it, rather than the nick of it." This morning he sat by his window, looking out upon the frost covered lawn thinking, "perhaps this morning I won't shave at all. Perhaps this morning I won't shave at all."

The Half Way Covenant

"HAVE YOU EVER SEEN Little Orphan Annie? No? Well she had curly hair like that, but not really. Sort of red and wavy. I suppose that would be a better way to describe it. Red and wavy. And there was a certain voluptuousness about her. An exuberance and enthusiasm that was contagious. Yet, there seemed to be something insincere, too. She was an infatuation for everyone and a colleague to none."

"When did she arrive?" he asked.

"In the summer. Right after the last tornado. Well, maybe she was the last, the last tornado. She took the place by storm beginning with that very first day when a few of us drove down to the station to greet her. To get her. Pick her up. She doesn't drive, you know."

"Yes. But go ahead. Continue. I need to know. Tell me about that first day. First and last days. They're the important ones. Right?"

"Maybe? I'm not sure. We'll see."

"But go on with the story. At the station, what happened there?"

"Oh, yeah. Right. The station. Well, we didn't say anything to each other then. Not till later, but we all felt something. Right away. We didn't speak to each other. We didn't look at each other. She was the focus of everything right from the start. You see, after we parked the car and went inside we were struck, all of us, man or woman. Maybe at first it was just surprise. Surprise, amazement, wonder. There she was, her hair aflame, almost, in the middle of the dark, run-down station with twenty or thirty teenage girls all about her. She was the center, the sun in that damp place and these girls in

Catholic school uniforms – the tie shoes and knee highs, the plaid kilts, white shirts, and plaid vests – seemed to maneuver for a closer position to her. Her brilliant hair contrasted so with the somber plaid of their uniforms, the dull, smoky gray of the walls. Some of the girls closest jumped up and down and brushed up against her. A strange sight, but we immediately behaved even more strangely, forced our way through the crowd, introduced ourselves, dragged her out to there. It wasn't a rescue. Maybe something more like a competition. Every person there wanted the prize to him or herself. Oblivious to all others. This we realized later.

"When we got her to the car the competition for her attention continued. Who would she grace with a word, a smile, a nod, an acknowledgment of any kind. That was the contest, though no one even noticed this at that point. Not till later. She was making us act like selfish children, you see.

"I remember once during a party at the Dean's house we were sitting outside on the terrace and then all of a sudden out of the forest that begins at the end of the Dean's yard came these young women dressed for parts in *A Midsummer Night's Dream* and they danced for her. Each one vying for her attention, each one willing to offer herself to her.

"Oh, don't get me wrong, Catholic girls and dancers. No, it wasn't just women who wanted her. Men, too, fawned, hovered about her. Like a bunch of worker bees about the hive. Drone on. New Salem Beach, California had never seen anything like this before. It was a kind of hysteria. Instead of the McCarthy era it was the Emily Burns era. All ours. The students loved her, the faculty loved her, the administration loved her, the staff loved her, everyone loved her and everyone wanted to love her. It went on like this for a year."

"So, what happened? I need to know."

"Well, her position was just for the year, a visiting appointment, and when a regular appointment opened up she applied, but she didn't get the job. That's all."

"Wait a second. What about the love everybody felt for her? How couldn't she get the job?"

"Well, you see, it went to Thomas Richards instead."

"Richards!"

"Yes. The committee decided …"

"But nobody likes Richards."

"Nobody dislikes him, either. Keeps pretty much to himself. Besides, you'd never find a harder worker than Richards. Anywhere. He's here every day: morning, noon, and night."

"I don't understand."

"Well, of course, everyone wanted Emily. But after extensive and intense discussion … Well, you see."

"No. I don't."

"Richards is so devoted to his work. He's such a hard worker."

"Did he take the place by storm?"

"Well, no. He's too quiet for that. Behind the scenes and very, very sincere. I'd almost say devout about his work, if it wasn't such an awkward thing to say."

"You have said it. And awkwardly, too. All of it. This. I don't get it. So tell me, how's his driving?"

"What? Oh, funny. Straight as an arrow."

"No doubt. No doubt. Hey, first and last days, right? You told me about her first day, but not about her last. So tell me. Give me a better conclusion. Something brighter than the above."

"Ок. The last day. Well, here goes. Before we drove her back to the station we had a going away party for her. Not a big affair, just some of the graduate students and people in the department. That sort of thing. Not too different from this one, but much more distracting. Richards was there by then and unlike the rest of us he didn't make Emily the focus of his attention. It was hard to get him away from his work. Even then. Even right after his arrival. Right to work. Work, work, work. He was polite, though. It must have been a bit awkward for him. Everyone knew that they had both applied for the same job. She was charming as ever, captivating. He seemed a little agitated, though polite. We figured he looked upon this party as an interruption in his work, but felt obligated to be there. At one point I saw him take a potato chip and put it in the dip. It broke and he seemed to curse or something. Meanwhile she had moved next to him and he turned, saw her and she reached down, took his broken half of the chip out of the dip and ate it, all the while looking right at him, in his eyes. I could hear him say – obviously irritated – 'excuse me,' and he left. Then she said her goodbyes and we were gone, too, off to the station. On the way out we passed Richards's office and could hear him typing away madly. She started to laugh just then, a wild, primitive, out-of-control belly laugh and we joined her though we didn't quite know why. A short time later she waved goodbye to us from the window of her departing train. We stood there for a moment or two after the train left and then without a word, in silence we returned to the university and we returned to work, the spell broken, and that my friend was the last day."

"I feel like I'm missing something important here. Something about the committee and its charge perhaps?"

"So you're looking for what it all means?"

"Yes. If I can figure it out, then I'll be about to figure out how to fit in here and my tenure at New Salem State will be assured. This I do believe, indeed."

"Simple as that?"

"Simple as that."

"Well then, my ephebe, it's as simple as this. He's written four books, one of over a thousand pages, and she's written a mere two, one of less than two-hundred pages. This is what it all means, pages and nothing more. Words and nothing less. That's our business, after all. Now get to work. The party's over."

POTES & POETS PRESS PUBLICATIONS

Bruce Andrews, *Executive Summary*, $9.00
Dennis Barone, *Echoes*, $14.00
Dennis Barone, *Forms / Froms*, $7.00
D. Barone / P. Ganick, eds., *The Art of Practice: 45 Contemporary Poets*, $18.00
Martine Bellen, *Places People Dare Not Enter*, $8.00
Steve Benson, *Reverse Order*, $9.00
Paul Buck, *no title*, $8.00
O. Cadiot / C. Bernstein, *Red, Green & Black*, $8.00
Abigail Child, *A Motive for Mayhem*, $8.50
A. Clarke / R. Sheppard, eds., *Floating Capital*, $12.00
Norma Cole, *Contrafact*, $10.50
Norma Cole, *Metamorphopsia*, $8.50
Cid Corman, *Root Song*, $7.50
Beverly Dahlen, *A Reading (11–17)*, $8.50
Tina Darragh, *a(gain)2st the odds*, $8.00
D. Davidson / T. Mandel, *Absence Sensorium*, $14.00
Jean Day, *The I and the You*, $11.00
Ray DiPalma, *The Jukebox of Memnon*, $8.50
Ray DiPalma, *Provocations*, $11.00
Rachel Blau DuPlessis, *Drafts xi–xxx, the Fold*, $12.00
Rachel Blau DuPlessis, *Drafts 3–14*, $9.50
Rachel Blau DuPlessis, *Tabula Rosa*, $8.50
Theodore Enslin, *Case Book*, $8.50
Norman Fischer, *The Devices*, $7.00
Peter Ganick, *Rectangular Morning Poem*, $9.00
Michael Gottlieb, *River Road*, $10.00
Jessica Grim, *Locale*, $10.00
Carla Harryman, *Vice*, $7.50
P. Inman, *Think of One*, $7.50
Sheila E. Murphy, *Falling In Love Falling In Love With You Syntax*, $16.50
Susan Smith Nash, *Catfishes and Jackals*, $12.00
Melanie Neilson, *Natural Facts*, $10.50
Gil Ott, *Public Domain*, $8.50
Maureen Owen, *Untapped Maps*, $9.50
Stephen Ratcliffe, *spaces in the light said to be where one/ comes from*, $9.50

Kit Robinson, *The Champagne of Concrete*, $9.00
Leslie Scalapino, *Goya's L.A.*, $8.50
Leslie Scalapino, *How Phenomena Appear to Unfold*, $9.00
Spencer Selby, *House of Before*, $9.00
Ron Silliman, *Lit*, $7.50
Ron Silliman, *Toner*, $9.50
Diane Ward, *Imaginary Movie*, $9.50

Potes & Poets also publishes A.BACUS, a single-author newsletter, eight times a year; a series of Limited Editions, called Extras; fifteen chapbooks issued during 1981 and 1982; and, POTEPOETZINE and POTEPOETTEXT, electronic texts available free by sending an e-mail address to: potepoet@home.com.

Please write to us at:
Potes & Poets Press Inc
181 Edgemont Avenue
Elmwood CT 06110-1005 USA
And: potepoet@home.com
For a complete catalog and ordering information.